THE GRAND ONES OF SAN ILDEFONSO

A small border town in New Mexico, San Ildefonso had survived a lot. Marauding Indians, lawless *bandoleros,* soldiers in blue and raiders in war paint had come and gone. But now, renegades from south of the border were attempting to seize the village itself, in search of rumoured *conquistador* treasure. Lázaro Guardia, agent for the Forthright Stage & Freight Company, leads defence. With few young men to conscript, the village women and even the priest take up arms. The answer may be an old cannon, housed for years in the mission ... but is there someone among the villagers who knows how to aim and fire?

THE GRAND ONES OF SAN ILDEFONSO

THE GRAND ONES OF SAN ILDEFONSO

by

Lauran Paine

The Golden West Large Print Books
Long Preston, North Yorkshire,
BD23 4ND, England.

British Library Cataloguing in Publication Data.

Paine, Lauran
    The grand ones of San Ildefonso.

    A catalogue record of this book is
    available from the British Library

    ISBN   978-1-84262-959-8 pbk

Published in Large Print 2014 by arrangement with
Golden West Literary Agency

The Golden West Large Print is an imprint of Library Magna
Books Ltd.

Printed and bound in Great Britain by
T.J. (International) Ltd., Cornwall, PL28 8RW

Chapter One

A Separate Land

In the south desert country water mattered. This was something that had been known for a thousand years. It was not possible to create houses, sheds, even corrals and churches, without water to make adobe bricks, to provide something for animals and people to drink.

Where there was water there had long been people. Indians used the term Anasazi – meaning the old ones – to signify the original settlers where there was water. Later settlers – Spaniards and their emulators, *mestizo* Mexicans – used different names, meaning approximately the same thing. The old ones, the first people to congregate where there was water.

What became New Mexico Territory after Mexico's defeat by the United States in 1848 had remained isolated from areas and events elsewhere. People residing in a world of marginal survival had no concern for grand events, beginning with Spain's earlier conquest and ending with conquest by the United States. The raising of a new flag, called by Mexicans *the bloody gridiron,* caused no particular problem.

Mud bricks could not be made of flags. For that purpose water was needed. Marauding Indians, bands of lawless *bandoleros,* soldiers in blue, raiders in rags, killers in war paint came and went while such villages as San Ildefonso remained. Because mud structures did not burn, because residents of such villages had little worth stealing, and because change and grand events were meaningless compared to survival, San Ildefonso yielded possessions – mostly horses, mules, and burros – with fatalistic resignation. It could be stated as a fact that the isolated hamlets of New Mexico that had survived a thousand years would survive another thousand years.

San Ildefonso's *Catolica* sanctuary had three stories. The bell tower, that had once held a bell, now held the discarded refuse of centuries. San Ildefonso's mission was old. A fat little brass cannon, belonging to Juan de Oñate's colonizing expedition, had once fired at the cross atop the church. It was a near miss. Afterwards for two hundred years that ocotillo symbol of the true faith had listed several degrees to the west.

San Ildefonso's irregular plaza was a dusty place. The old well, bricked up waist high to prevent dogs, children, and even burros from falling in, had been an unfailing source of water for centuries. The houses, small, rude with walls three feet thick, had loopholes facing outward. Indians – Kiowas, Comanches, Apaches, even Yaquis and Zapotecs – up out of Mexico raided, and this was not to mention fleeing bands of desperate rebels of failed revolutions southward in Mexico who, in their own land, were shot out of hand.

The most recent raid on San Ildefonso had resulted in no deaths and so was a genuine novelty. It had been made by ragged men on foot, seeking saddle animals. It had been successfully accomplished at two o'clock in the morning.

It was useless to track the thieves who had ridden the stolen animals back down into Mexico – at the most a hard day's ride – because overtaking the thieves in their own territory had been done before with a unique result: neither the stolen animals nor the men who went after them were seen again. With one exception.

Three days later one animal returned, a burro belonging to the parish priest, Father Damion Sanchez, who, going outside in the early morning, was met by his burro whose expression of reproach lingered even after the good *padre* had put him in his shed and fed him a liberal mangerful of cured grass.

It was the opinion of Moses Morisco, owner of the general store, that the new owners of the land, *Los Estados Unidos*, should be responsible for enforcing the law

9

and providing protection to the people. His most recent statement to this effect was made in the *cantina,* and the very dark, squatty, and barrel-chested proprietor, Juan Bohorquez, laughed so loudly bottles on his back-bar shelves rattled.

'The United States doesn't even know we are here,' Juan Bohorquez explained. 'When the soldiers patrol, they are the signal. When they are miles past, the raiders come and are gone before the soldiers make their return.'

'So,' said the storekeeper, Moses Morisco, 'we are to do nothing?'

'Exactly. That is what we've been doing since you and I had moss stuffed in our diapers.' Bohorquez could not permit this opportunity to pass so easily, so he added: 'The next time they might raid your store and take everything ... the tinned food, the dried beans, the bolts of cloth ... everything.'

Moses Morisco considered his lined and weathered face in the back-bar mirror. 'They would need a wagon,' he said. He put a small coin beside his empty glass and returned to the store, which he had locked when he had left, and which he unlocked when he returned.

The time was approaching for San Ildefonso's *el dia de los muertos* when a solemn procession trooped to the cemetery that was located north and east of the church. The day of the dead was to honor those departed. Elsewhere such a day was commemorated with flowers. San Ildefonso had very few flowers, especially in the late summer, so people brought little cakes and prayer beads, ticking off each bead as Father Damion swung the censer, prayed, and called for divine favor.

It was in the evening of the day of the dead – with the dying day marked by a red sun, settling low in the west – that Isabel Montenegro sat in shade, separating peas from their pods. She commented to her neighbor, Francesca Cardinál: 'There were two strangers. Did you notice them?'

'No.'

'Unwashed, unshaven, wearing guns. They were hungry.'

'Men are always hungry, for one thing or another.'

'I saw them after we returned from the cemetery. I pointed them out to Lázaro Guardia. He said they could be *arrieros*. But there were no pack mules in the public corral.'

'Why do you worry?'

Isabel Montenegro finished with the peas. While putting the pans aside, she said: 'There has been another revolution down below.'

Francesca Cardinál shrugged. 'There are always revolutions. You think the strangers might be fleeing?'

11

'*¿Quién sabe?* Tomorrow I go look for them. Tonight my José will sleep with his pistol.'

Francesca Cardinál said nothing. Isabel's husband, José, sleeping with a pistol would be a novelty. He usually slept with a head full of tequila.

With the arrival of summer, the desert flowers died. Small animals moved closer to the village where foraging was better, and the most precious commodity – more precious than gold – might be placed outside for small animals, or it might not. With the arrival of summer there was a general preoccupation with water. It came out of the ground south of San Ildefonso and had been channeled to the village through an *acequia*. Because it was the custom to take a *siesta* during the burning heat of the day, the residents of San Ildefonso had supper between eight and nine o'clock at night.

In early spring stockmen drove herds south, and, as soon as the graze and browse began to cure, they drove their cattle back northward. It was a ritual almost as old as the settlement itself. For the most part the stockmen now were *gringos* who brought their own riders. Between owners and riders a seasonal lift was given the settlement, particularly in the case of Morisco's store, the only establishment of its kind for a hundred miles in any direction.

The same applied to the *cantina*. *Gringo* stockmen were hearty drinkers. They did not mingle well with the natives, but that was something that worked both ways. Even the *vaqueros* of San Ildefonso seemed to share little with their *gringo* counterparts from up north.

The free-grazers had been gone some time before full summer heat arrived. San Ildefonso settled back into routines as it had for generations. With the departure of the high country stockmen the people of San Ildefonso reverted. Moses Morisco 'rent his garments' over unpaid bills and accounts in arrears. He could not, he lamented to all who would listen, maintain an inventory unless he was paid. No one denied this, but, as God knew, without more than a survival income, payment must defer to miracles, which unfortunately did not occur often in the south desert country. Chickens, eggs, and the surplus produce of garden patches did occur, but, as Moses Morisco said often, how many chickens can a man eat, how many pounds of black-eyed peas does one need for stews, and the small, mottled ears of Indian corn, fine for tortillas and *entomotados*, while made edible with the meat of wild pigs, were something Moses Morisco would not touch. The barter system, that had been the mainstay of southern desert communities since time out of mind, worked well. However, when Moses Morisco ordered replenishment supplies, the sellers required cash, not chickens.

All of this the townsmen understood but could do little to alleviate. Even mustang hunters whose occasional forays provided money, usually in small amounts of silver, contributed little. Wild horse hunting was not always successful, and now, with *soldados norteamericanos* patrolling the land and with *gringo* law and order fully established, it was not like the old days – highwaymen, thieves of animals, robbers of all kinds who bought supplies in border communities while making a run for safety in Mexico no longer appeared.

Two brothers, Lázaro and Epifanio Guardia, maintained a large mud corral and a much smaller way station office for the Forthright Stage & Freight Company whose headquarters was in Santa Fé. Forthright stages visited San Ildefonso about once a month – only when there was enough mail or light freight or passengers to warrant the expense of the trip. The brothers were respected. They had steady salaries, something others in San Ildefonso rarely had. In fact, Lázaro had been elected *alcalde* – the *gringos* called it mayor – twelve years earlier, and each subsequent year had been reaffirmed in office. The community's business was conducted in the small way station building.

Summer was passing when Epifanio, constable as well as horse wrangler for the Forthright Company, made a discovery that brought the dozing community to life. He had found six horses branded U S on the neck. They wore saddles and bridles. The reins had been stepped on and broken by half their length. He brought the horses to the corral where it was observed that each animal had severe galls.

The elfin Efraim Montoya was summoned. He was the community doctor. He treated animals as well as people. The wizened old man said the horses had been wandering at least several weeks. When he asked about their riders, all he got were shrugs.

Epifanio and Lázaro went out the following day to backtrack. It was very hot and, had they not had canteens, they would have suffered even more. But canteens did not service horses, and their mounts began to droop about the time they breasted a scrub-brush land swell and stopped stone still.

Lázaro hastily crossed himself. 'Six,' he said.

His brother was already turning his horse when he spoke. 'The flies. They've been down there a long time.'

When they reached San Ildefonso and reported what they had found, Father Damion – who had named his Mexican burro *Señor Satán* because, although he weighed less than

15

eight hundred pounds, he would fight other mules or horses with the tenacity of his namesake – said he would ride out to see for himself. Meanwhile, he suggested, someone should ride to Fort Sedgewick, thirty miles southwest, and inform the Army. He also said he would require volunteers to provide Christian burials for the dead soldiers.

Two youths volunteered for the ride to the fort. Volunteers for the burial of six corpses that had been cooking in the sun for several weeks was another matter, until Juan Bohorquez, the *cantina* owner, solved the problem by agreeing to become one of the burial party and promising to supply four canteens of water as well as two bottles of tequila.

Father Damion required no directions except to ride westerly, which he did until a light breeze arrived along with flies and circling *zopilotes*. Bohorquez established order. Each man's bandanna was soaked with water before being tied into place, and each grave-digger's weakening resolve was strengthened from the two bottles. Father Damion went down into the arroyo, bandanna tightly in place, and by force of a formidable will held back the inclination to be sick as he plundered the pockets of the dead. He also removed neck amulets. Three of the six dead soldiers had Saint Christopher medals. When he climbed out of the arroyo, Juan Bohorquez jerked his head and led the others down into the arroyo, where there was no breeze, and where Torres Mendoza, one of the volunteers from the village, promptly heaved up his boot straps.

The graves were barely deep enough. The burial party mounded dirt to complete the covering. It would always be clear to those appearing upon the rim of the arroyo that six graves were lower down.

It was sundown before Father Damion led the return, soundlessly working beads through his fingers, ignoring the men with him, and not completely finishing his prayers when San Ildefonso was in sight. The grave-diggers disappeared among the houses. Only Juan Bohorquez returned to his *cantina* to provide the grisly details of the burials. That evening he was paid for more drinks than would happen again until Christmas.

One week later the pair of youths who had gone to alert the Army returned with information that a full company of dragoons was following, and in fact the horse soldiers reached San Ildefonso the following mid-morning.

Father Damion told the rawboned, weathered, pale-eyed officer, Captain Frank Bonham, how to locate the arroyo. At the same time he presented the officer with a small box, containing articles he had retrieved before the soldiers were buried.

Captain Bonham had been seven years on

17

the south desert. His Spanish was without accent, but he used English almost exclusively on the grounds that, since the south desert no longer belonged to Mexico, its people should speak English. There was nothing wrong with the concept. It was just not a very successful one.

Father Damion spoke English. He used it after the dragoons had departed to tell Moses Morisco the captain had forcefully said he was aware of the degree of resentment people like those in San Ildefonso felt for *norteamericanos*, and that, as God was his witness, he would discover who had ambushed that patrol and would tie them by the wrists to the tail of wild horses.

Moses Morisco turned his hands palms up when he replied. '*Rurales* do that, not North Americans.'

Father Damion shrugged. 'Isabel Montenegro said there were two armed strangers at the ceremony on the day of the dead. Did you know that?'

The storekeeper had heard. 'Perhaps relatives of the dead?'

Father Damion accepted that, left the store, and, returning to his church, found Lázaro Guardia, waiting on a bench beneath the full-length overhang of the church's east side. Lázaro rose when the priest approached and held out one hand. A misshapen bullet lay on his palm.

Father Damion asked where it had come from, and Lázaro was pocketing the slug when he replied. 'It was under one of the soldiers. Do you know what caliber it is?'

'No. Do you?'

'*Si*. It came from a Sharps carbine. The kind those soldiers would have been carrying. But there were no guns, were there?'

Father Damion sat on the bench as he shook his head.

Lázaro also sat. 'Whoever ambushed them had Army guns.'

Father Damion turned his head, frowning. 'Other soldiers? Lázaro, *bandoleros* also have such guns. They are common on both sides of the border.'

'Yes. Tell me, Father, why did whoever killed those men use Army weapons ... why was it necessary?'

Father Damion eased back against the cool adobe wall. 'What are you saying?'

'Did you hear of two armed strangers at the ceremony on the day of the dead? Who were they, and why were they here?'

Father Damion ranged a look over the grave markers in the cemetery. Several had become tilted from age. He had meant to straighten them. 'They could have been here because they have relatives among the dead. I've known it to happen. Strangers come to offer prayers for long-dead relatives. And why wouldn't they be armed?'

19

'Father, those men did not stop at any grave. They ate and hardly spoke to the rest of us...'

'Lázaro, you are imagining things.'

'Possibly, but did you notice much about those men?'

'No, not much.'

'Their shirts were darker in some places than other places.'

'What are you talking about?' the priest wondered testily.

'Where their shirts were dark was the crossed place where bandoleers are commonly worn.'

Father Damion returned to his study of the tilted stones as he dryly said: 'Lázaro, come inside. It is hot out here. I have some very good wine the bishop sent me last year.'

Chapter Two

Epifanio

The detail of soldiers returned late in the afternoon, dehydrated and solemn as owls. Captain Bonham went to the corral-yard office, tugged off his gauntlets, folded them under and over his belt. He looked steadily at Lázaro, who gestured toward the hanging *olla*. The officer drank deeply, which made more sweat burst out, sat down, and said: 'I think they were shot by their own weapons.' At Lázaro's expression of wonderment the officer spoke again. He was an old trooper, hard as iron and spare with words. 'We followed tracks south, but they were old marks, and there were other tracks. *Bandoleros* as sure as I'm sitting here. My question is ... how could raiders like that set up an ambush?'

Lázaro spread his hands. The idea was plain to him. It had happened many times. 'They hate *gringo* soldiers.'

'But by my figuring, they talked their way right up to the soldiers. Were very close, maybe sharing water, when the killing began. And why didn't they catch the horses? Mex raiders always go for the horses. Horses are more important to them than guns.'

Lázaro faintly frowned. 'Do you have answers to your questions?'

'No, but I thought you might help.'

'How?'

'You have people here who go down over the line. Relatives, friends, traders. They could find out how that massacre happened.'

Lázaro nodded. It was a fact that most of San Ildefonso's residents often went down into Mexico. There were relatives down there as well as friends. 'I will try,' he told the captain, who rose to his full, sinewy height.

'They had a revolution a couple of months back,' Bonham pursued the subject.

'Yes, but the fleeing defeated did not come here. Maybe they went past in the night. I don't know, but we weren't raided, as is the custom.' Lázaro thought of something. 'A few days back at our ceremony for the dead there were two strangers.' He shrugged. What he had just said sounded foolish to him. 'San Ildefonso is a small place. Everyone knows everyone else, but not those two. Unshaven, faded-looking, armed men.'

'They are gone?'

'Yes. They did not stay to eat after the ceremony.' Lázaro rose. 'Father Damion said they probably had relatives at the graveyard and had come for the ceremony when everyone remembers and prays for the dead.'

22

Captain Bonham went to the door, gazed dispassionately at people passing, turned, and said: 'I'll come back in a week or two. That will give you time to get information. *Adiós.*'

Lázaro nodded, sat back down, and was still at his desk when his brother arrived. Epifanio was a mild man, friendly, good-natured, unlike Lázaro who was thoughtful and practical.

He mentioned the soldiers. Lázaro told him what had been said. Epifanio sat, pushed his legs out, and considered scuffed old boots as he spoke. 'Torres Mendoza's old mother lives down there. Do you want me to talk to him?'

Lázaro was briefly thoughtful before nodding. Torres Mendoza was a shrewd man. He traded southward as often as he could. If there was anything to be found out, Torres Mendoza would be able to do it.

After Epifanio departed, Lázaro went out into the corral yard. For some unfathomable reason he was uneasy. The more he thought about the captain's visit, the more uneasy he became. He was in the alley out back when the wizened Efraim Montoya appeared, carrying two chickens, his pay for delivering a girl baby. The old man eyed Lázaro Guardia with snake-like intensity before he said: 'Do you know the people who now live in the old abandoned house of the Garcias?'

Lázaro nodded. He knew them. They were

young and raised a huge vegetable garden. The woman's name was Estralita; her man's name was Jacobo. Their last name escaped him.

Efraim said – 'It was a fine baby girl' – and continued to stare intently. He held up the chickens. 'Two for a girl, five for a boy.' Efraim shrugged. 'Boys will work. Girls' – another shrug – 'have more babies.'

Lázaro had known the old *curandero* since childhood. Only God could say how old Efraim was, and about such things He was traditionally silent.

'Why are you standing there, staring at me?' Lázaro asked.

The old man had trouble standing for long periods and looked around for something to sit on. There was nothing. He shifted his weight to the leg that bothered him the least before saying: 'They have a guest.'

Lázaro's impatience was mounting, so he was sharp with Efraim. 'It happens, even in San Ildefonso.'

'Yes, of course, it does, but this man they keep in a tiny storeroom. I could hear him groaning. I asked if he needed curing, and Jacobo said he fell in some rocks and hurt himself, but he would be fine in a few days.' Efraim's black, intent stare never wavered. 'There was pink water in a bucket and some bloody rags.'

Lázaro's brows gathered into a frown, but

24

he said nothing, so Efraim finished what he had to say. 'If he fell in some rocks, he must also have shot himself because there was a bullet on a little table. I think he has been visiting for several weeks, and that would be about the time the soldiers were killed.'

Efraim's good leg was now aching. He nodded and limped past, carrying his brace of chickens.

Lázaro watched the *curandero* go for a short time, then went back to his corral-yard office. He was buckling the shell belt and pistol around his middle about the time his brother entered, stopped dead still, and raised his eyebrows. Lázaro pushed past him without a word.

He recalled the name of the people who now resided in the *jacal* formerly lived in by the Garcias. Their name was Obregón.

When Jacobo opened the door, his eyes widened. Lázaro lied with a clear conscience. He told Obregón he had come to welcome their new daughter and pushed his way inside.

Estralita Obregón came from a small, dark room. At sight of Lázaro's armament she went pale. He asked about the baby. While she answered, Jacobo moved near another small room where there was no door; instead there was a hanging purple cloth with improbably large cabbage roses on it. The Obregóns were young. Jacobo had been hauling faggots since the pair of them had taken over the Garcia house. Lázaro knew little about Jacobo except that he had two burros, was large and muscular with the fair complexion of a *gachupín*.

They offered squash cut into squares and sweetened by soaking it in sugar water. Lázaro accepted, but neither of the Obregóns ate. He made talk, something his brother was better at, and was beginning to squirm through long silences when what sounded like a puppy whimpered in the room Jacobo Obregón was guarding. Lázaro chewed the candy, swallowed, and asked if there were a sick dog in the room behind Jacobo because, if there was, he who cared for dogs might be able to help.

Jacobo wiped sweat off his face on a sleeve before saying they had no dog.

Lázaro considered the larger, younger man. 'What was it, then, that I heard?'

Jacobo started to speak when the sound came again. This time Lázaro brushed past him to pull the drape aside.

The man looking up at him from a wall bunk was soaked with sweat. He was naked from the waist up, and there was a cumbersome bandage around his chest. The right side showed blood.

Lázaro turned, eyed Estralita and Jacobo, and turned to enter the small, dark room for a closer look. There was a chair in one corner.

Clothing was draped upon it. There was also a shell belt and holstered Colt. Leaning to one side of the chair was a stubby Sharps carbine.

Lázaro spoke to Jacobo without looking away from the flushed wet face of the man on the bunk. 'He needs the *curandero*. He is your relative?' When there was no answer, he asked another question. 'How did he get hurt?' This time he faced around. There was no longer any sign of Estralita, but Jacobo filled the doorway. 'How?'

Jacobo made a slightly deprecating gesture with both hands. 'I don't know. My woman and I went for a moonlight walk. He was out there ... like that.'

'How long ago did you go for this walk?'

'The day I am unsure. About ten days ago.' Jacobo drifted his gaze to the wounded man. 'Sometimes he says things that don't make sense. Other times he only says we must get him a horse.' Jacobo made that slight gesture again. 'He couldn't stay on a horse one *vara*.'

'You brought him here and have been caring for him?'

'Yes.'

'What name does he use?'

'Ask him.'

Lázaro faced the bunk and leaned slightly as he asked in Spanish what the man's name was and got a shock. The reply came in accentless English.

27

'John Smith.'

Lázaro straightened up. 'How do you happen to be here, *Señor* Smith?'

This time the wounded man faced the wall and did not speak. As Lázaro was leaving the room, John Smith said one word. 'Water.'

Jacobo got the water. Lázaro stood in the doorway, watching Jacobo lift John Smith so he could drink.

Estralita came from her child's room and softly said: 'We know only that we found him and brought him here to be cared for.'

Lázaro had a question. 'For how much money, *señora?*'

Jacobo answered from the wounded man's doorway. 'Fifteen *gringo* dollars ... and this.'

Lázaro glanced at the ham-sized hand that held a very old, ornate crucifix of solid gold with inlaid gem stones. He knew nothing of such objects, but as he took it and hefted it, he said: 'Heavy. Was he wearing this?'

'No. It was in his pocket.'

'What did he say about it?'

'Nothing.'

As Lázaro pocketed the crucifix and looked steadily at the larger young man, he said: 'Father Damion knows about such things. I'll send the *curandero*. Don't move him.'

Jacobo nodded, and Lázaro left the house, walking toward the north end of town in the direction of the church. He had formed a suspicion before leaving the Obregón *jacal*.

28

He found the priest, sitting under the over-hang on the east side of the church. Although they nodded at each other, Lázaro did not say a word as he held out the crucifix.

Father Damion's eyes widened. He took the cross, turned it over and back, hefted it, and looked up. 'Where did you get this?'

Lázaro answered truthfully as he sat down on the same bench. Father Damion held the crucifix in one hand. 'It is very old,' he said. 'It is very valuable. Have you ever seen one like it?'

'No.'

'I have, in Mexico. They are treasured. The great cathedrals have them.' Father Damion turned the crucifix over and held it close to his face. 'Taxo,' he said. 'There, you see the silversmith's mark and that tiny symbol. It was made in Taxo, possibly a hundred years ago.' Father Damion held the crucifix in his lap. 'During the uprisings there is always plundering. Holy places, too. Tell me about this man who had it.'

There was little to say that Lázaro had not already said, but he speculated. 'I think he is a *bandolero*. How he was shot I have no idea. Father, you should go see him.'

'He is hurt badly?'

Lázaro nodded solemnly. 'It is the smell,' he said.

The priest rose. The smell of infection preceded death. As he pocketed the crucifix, he nodded and walked the length of the overhang, stepped from ancient brick into dust, and kept on walking.

Lázaro returned to the way station and was told by a youngster that his brother, Epifanio, had gone riding on one of the Mexican mules.

Isabel Montenegro came into the shade of the corral yard, seeking Lázaro Guardia. He was slouched in thought in the small office when she entered. Her arrival startled him. As he straightened in the chair, the dark, plump woman stood erectly with hands clasped across her middle. She said: 'It is something.'

He regarded her stonily. *'¿Quién?'*

'I don't know, but it is something. One of those strangers was in the store when I went for dried fruit. He was talking to Moses Morisco.'

'One of the strangers who was at the cemetery?'

She nodded primly. 'Certainly.'

'And he was alone?'

'As far as I know, he was alone. Lázaro, you are the *alcalde*. Epifanio is the constable. It is the duty of both of you to know things.'

Lázaro rose, swept up his hat, and headed for the door, leaving the *señora* standing with clasped hands.

The storekeeper was weighing dried apples

for the woman who cooked for Torres Mendoza. There would have been gossip, except that the woman was not only a widow but had a very pronounced mustache along with being heavily scarred from the pox.

Lázaro brushed the brim of his hat as the woman passed, carrying her purchases, and Moses stood behind his counter, gazing dispassionately at his only other patron.

Lázaro asked about a stranger at the store, and Moses Morisco made a fluttery hand gesture as he explained. 'A *gachupín*. Polite and agreeable. We talked of store business. He once had a relative in Matamoras who ran a store. He was interested in how long it took me to get supplies from Santa Fé. He said his name was Joáquin Otero. He was passing through. He had been down in Mexico and was now going north. Pleasant to talk to. God knows, it was a relief. He understood being unable to collect, and that wholesalers will only deal with those who send cash with their orders.'

Lázaro leaned on the counter. 'He was one of those two strangers at the ceremony in the cemetery?'

'No. Who said that?'

'Would you recognize those two?'

'Certainly. They bought tobacco from me. No, this stranger wasn't a *mestizo*. He looked like a genuine *peninsular*. A Spaniard, not a Mexican.'

31

Lázaro searched for another who had seen the mannerly, pleasant wearer of spurs, the *gachupín,* and encountered only one other individual who had spoken to him. Juan Bohorquez had served the stranger wine, two glasses of it, and they had visited. The man had appeared about noon when the *cantina* had only two other customers, both old men, asleep in chairs by the window.

What did they talk about? The weather, of course. Everyone started conversations with the weather. Otherwise the soft-spoken and friendly *gachupín* had been interested in how often stages and freighters came to San Ildefonso.

Bohorquez gave the bar top a wide, vigorous sweep with a moist rag before continuing. And he smiled. 'I told him stages rarely come and freighters never, unless they have good reason. He said he had been to the store, and its shelves appeared to be well stocked. I said that was about the extent of freighting this close to the border.'

Lázaro went in search of Isabel Montenegro, found her in a chair on the shaded verandah of the Cardinál house with Francesca Cardinál. After bowing to Francesca, he told Isabel that she must have been mistaken. It hadn't been one of those rough strangers who had visited the store. It had been a *gachupín*.

The sturdy woman stiffened where she

sat. 'I recognized him. He was one of those dirty, unshaven strangers. One was in the alley behind the store, holding two horses. I saw *him* enter and leave the store.'

Lázaro left the two women, returned to the small corral-yard office, and lighted a crooked, very dark Mexican cigar. Not everyone could handle them, but Lázaro could. He did not smoke often, but he had been smoking since his teens.

Of course, strangers had every right to visit San Ildefonso. In fact, if they spent money there and departed, local residents had only charitable thoughts about them. And no one could imagine strangers arriving, and staying, in San Ildefonso. Occasionally someone would arrive and linger, but never for long.

He stepped outside to gauge the time by the slant of the sun. It was getting close to sundown. He went back inside to await Epifanio's return.

It was a very long wait. In fact, although the Mexican mule returned some time in the night, it was three days before some youthful mustangers found Epifanio. They returned to town without him, hunted up Lázaro, and related what they had seen. Epifanio, a diffident, kindly, well-thought-of individual was dead. One bullet from behind, high up. Lázaro hitched up a light wagon, took along an old roll of wagon canvas, and followed the directions of the mustangers.

Epifanio was face down. He was swelling. Lázaro wrapped him, put him in the wagon bed, then he examined the area, moving slowly back and forth until he found the spent casing, reflecting sunlight, behind a squatty thorn-pin bush. He also saw where the ambushers' horses had stood for a long time in a dry wash not far from the site where Epifanio was lying face down.

Lázaro sighted from the place of the brass casing. His brother had been riding toward town, in an easterly direction. The bullet that had killed him had come from a thicket slightly southward and in a westerly direction.

Lázaro pocketed the casing, turned back in the direction of San Ildefonso, allowed the horse to have its head, and speculated. He rummaged through an assortment of reasons for his brother to have made his last ride and found nothing logical or believable, but there was one element that remained after the others had been discarded. His brother had been bushwhacked less than a mile from the arroyo where the soldiers had been massacred.

It was dark by the time he got back. He put up the horse, left the light rig in the center of the runway, and went out to the church to pray for his brother. They had been close since orphaned childhood. Lázaro had squirmed for Epifanio a number of times when his brother had been cursed and scorned without fighting back. He had owned an excellent Colt revolver and never carried it.

After prayers Lázaro returned to the gloom of the eastern wall of the ancient church and sat in silence, trying to imagine who had killed his brother from behind. Not only who, but why?

He eventually went to the mud-walled bunkhouse set against the northwest wall of the corral yard where he and his brother had lived since hiring on with the Forthright company as operators of the San Ildefonso way station. Moonlight shone upon the empty bunk. Lázaro lay down, turned his back, but sleep would not come. It did not come even after sunrise.

Chapter Three

Caught!

In a place no larger than San Ildefonso the shock of Epifanio Guardia's murder was enough to keep both the store and the saloon closed one full day. The indignation encouraged a group of men who owned horses and mules to scour the countryside. They found nothing. Torres Mendoza, who had been absent during this time, returned late at night, cared for his animal before going to the corral yard, and kicked at the bunkhouse door until Lázaro opened it with a candle in one hand, his pistol in the other. Torres brushed past the gun, poured red wine from a jug into a tin cup, and half emptied it before looking around. Lázaro put both the candle and the revolver atop the scarred, old bunkhouse table, sat down. While jutting his chin in the direction of the empty bunk, Torres Mendoza said: 'Where is Epifanio?'

'Dead. Shot from behind not very far from where those soldiers were killed.'

'When?'

'We found him two days ago. We buried

him yesterday.' Lázaro poured another tin cup half full from the jug but did not raise it. He looked steadily across the table. 'What did you learn south of the border?'

'Have you ever heard of the Mejias?'

'No.'

'One was executed for making a *grito* for a new rebellion. They caught and shot him. It is a large family. Now another one, Sixto Mejia, is organizing for another rebellion. But this time the armies will earn their pay. Mejia is a veteran of many uprisings. Already he has men marching as far as the country south of us.'

Lázaro nodded. 'About the dead soldiers?'

Torres Mendoza's enthusiasm waned. 'I learned little. It was said the soldiers were where they shouldn't have been.'

'What does that mean?'

'*¿Quién sabe?* Down there the land is boiling.'

Lázaro gazed steadily at Torres Mendoza, wagging his head. 'Epifanio was shot in the back not far from where the soldiers died,' he repeated.

Mendoza looked shocked this time. Of the two Guardias he had liked Epifanio the best. 'Who shot him?'

'I don't know, but if you want me to guess, I would say that part of the territory has become dangerous for some reason I don't know.'

37

Mendoza made a wide gesture with both arms. 'There is nothing ... rattlesnakes, scorpions, gila monsters, dirt, and thorny brush.'

Lázaro could have agreed. Instead he said: 'Six *gringo* soldiers and my brother. There has to be a reason.'

Mendoza left the small office, wearing a long face. He would genuinely miss Epifanio Guardia.

The elfin *curandero* appeared in Lázaro's doorway, snakelike, very dark eyes bright. 'The wounded man is dead. Jacobo will bury him. Lázaro, while he was dying, he said to me Mexico is rising. He was part of the *bandoleros* who killed the soldiers.'

'Did he say why they were killed?'

'Only that there is a trail that must be kept open. Those were his last words. I think he was part *gringo*. Would that matter?'

It did not matter to Lázaro Guardia. 'How is Jacobo's baby?'

'The Obregóns are leaving. Jacobo will come to you for something of his that you have.'

San Ildefonso, as with other communities in the area, had reason to worry. Also as with other communities San Ildefonso had a huge pile of dried faggots a mile or so from the hamlet. They would be set afire as a warning if raiders swarmed up out of Mexico. Earlier, those fires had been used to warn of Indian raids.

Juan Bohorquez had youths ride out to watch in the direction of the border. Revolutions were common. Usually they amounted to little more than drunken raids for plunder. This time people did not have to be told the danger was very great. Old men who usually went out with burros to gather faggots for stove wood banded together. Guns appeared. The younger men, who normally made a bare living by trapping *mesteños,* rode out armed to the gills. It was – as old Maria Alvarez said – like old times. When she had been a girl, it was Comanches and Kiowas. Mexican Indians, too, the Chiricahuas who lived on both sides of the border. For some reason Maria Alvarez seemed younger, more willing to recall grisly events and to pass them along. It compounded the communal agitation since people – the women, anyway – who listened to Maria's tales of horror did not sleep very well.

Maria Alvarez told Francesca Cardinál that her son had gone south to join the emancipation of Mexico from the ruling tyrant. Francesca passed this along to Isabel Montenegro who told Juan Bohorquez who swore a blue streak. The old woman's son owed him money, and he hadn't gone to Mexico. He was a wild horse hunter.

Among those protecting San Ildefonso and its people were Lázaro and Father Damion who rode westerly, each mounted on a mule. They rode considerable distances out of their way in order to utilize land swells, brushy topouts. As Lázaro had said, unless someone knew why that particular stretch of country was deadly, there would be more innocents who would ride to their deaths. Father Damion turned out to know ways of being unseen while riding that made Lázaro wonder if, perhaps, the priest had always been a holy man.

The heat was formidable. Their animals sweated even around the eyes. When they eventually halted in shade from spindly palo-verdes and dismounted to scan the country-side, they saw a slouching rider in the middle distance. There was no mistaking the tight trousers, the short jacket, the large hat, or the reflected sunlight off silver. Father Damion spoke to himself: 'Mexican.' Lázaro said nothing.

Whoever he was, he did not wear the crossed bandoleers of revolutionaries or raiders. He rode without haste. They watched him until he descended into an arroyo and did not come out the far side.

Father Damion pursed his lips. 'Where did he go?'

Lázaro answered thoughtfully: 'Due west is the arroyo of the dead soldiers. South a mile or two is where I found my brother. Father, we had better go back. Whatever it is, we are very close to it.'

It was good advice, but a little late. They turned and, using the same route of concealment, headed for San Ildefonso.

Neither spoke for a long time. They rode slowly to favor their animals and were crossing an open space between two low upthrusts when four horsemen came up over a low rim and halted. Each Mexican was heavily armed. Two even had machetes in saddle scabbards.

Father Damion breathed a prayer. Lázaro recognized none of the Mexicans. He raised his right hand, palm forward. The Mexicans sat like statues without returning the salute.

They blocked the route to San Ildefonso. One of them eventually urged his horse closer and called out in Spanish: 'Why are you here?'

Lázaro replied loudly. 'Looking for lost horses.'

The Mexicans laughed. Their spokesman rode closer, drew his belt gun without haste, and cocked it as he said: 'Turn about. Ride back the way you came. Do nothing foolish. Be tranquil and I will not shoot you.'

They turned back. Their captors kept their distance. Only their spokesman was close enough so that, when he spoke, he did not have to raise his voice. 'You are the priest from San Ildefonso,' he said. 'Your friend has the corral at the lower end of the village.'

Neither Lázaro nor the priest replied. Both were fully occupied with their own thoughts. That they would probably be killed seemed certain. *Why would marauders who had killed six soldiers be reluctant about killing a priest and his companion?*

The swarthy spokesman said: 'Halt! Get down and rest.' He spoke swiftly to one of his riders. The man peeled off in a lope, riding southwest.

The swarthy man offered a canteen. Neither captive accepted, so he drank deeply, wiped his mouth, and spoke in English. 'There are no lost horses out here. Tell me the truth. Why are you here?'

Father Damion faced the Mexican, who wore a golden crucifix on a neck chain. 'We live here. I am the parish priest.'

'*Sí*, I know who you are. I know your friend is the *alcalde*. Tell me! What are you riding out here for?'

Lázaro answered. 'My brother was shot in the back out here. We were looking for the place.'

The sweating dark man grinned. 'Your brother was shot south of here two miles.'

Lázaro gazed steadily at the Mexican. 'Why was he killed?'

'Sit in the shade of your horses. Be patient.'

Neither captive sat. The dark man shrugged, turned his horse, and hunkered in its shade. He had black eyes, a coarse mouth,

42

and a beak of a nose. He was clearly enjoying himself. His age was indeterminate. He was not tall but had a bull neck and the appearance of toughness and strength.

His companions also dismounted and turned their animals to provide shade. Occasionally they muttered among themselves in Spanish.

Lázaro concentrated on the dark man built like a bull. 'Do you know a Joáquin Otero?' he asked.

The hunkering man's eyes narrowed as he nodded. 'You know him?'

'He was in the store at San Ildefonso.'

Two riders, approaching at a lope, put an end to the waiting. One of them was the man who had been sent away. His companion was tall, fair except for black eyes and hair. When they dismounted, the tall man nodded, loosened the *cincha*, and faced the captives. The squatting dark man rose as he said: 'This one knows Joáquin Otero.' He smiled.

The tall man looked steadily at Lázaro. 'I don't remember you. I am Joáquin Otero. Where did we meet?'

They hadn't met. Moses Morisco had met the tall man who asked questions in his store. Lázaro avoided a direct reply. 'Is there a reason for us to be held?' he asked.

Joáquin Otero studied both captives before answering. '*Sí*, there is a reason.'

'Are we to be told?' Lázaro asked.

43

The light-complected man shook his head. 'What were you looking for when you came out here?'

The dark man grinned. 'For lost horses, he told me. There are no lost horses.'

Otero sighed and swatted at a gnat. He told the dark man to tie the prisoners on their horses, blindfold them, and lead their horses.

While this was being done, a third marauder appeared. He sat watching and finally addressed Otero in Spanish. 'It will be soon. An outrider came south to tell us. Maybe tomorrow night. Maybe earlier.'

The captives were led with marauders on both sides and one in back. Joáquin Otero ignored everyone until the scent of wood smoke was discernible, ordered the blindfolds removed, then he dropped back beside the priest to say: 'Father, *bandoleros* came up here some time back. They were attacked by soldiers.' Otero paused, watching Father Damion's face. What he saw there encouraged him to alter to a degree what he had said. 'The soldiers came over the edge of an arroyo where the border jumpers were camped. You understand that border jumpers have only enemies, no matter which side of the border they are on. These men, taken by surprise, were too quick with their weapons. They killed six soldiers.'

Father Damion and Lázaro regarded the

light-complected man stonily. He kneed his animal up ahead and did not speak to the captives again until they went down into a deep arroyo – almost a cañon – where smoke was rising from a cooking fire. Lázaro counted six Mexicans. Joáquin Otero spoke aside to a grizzled, graying man as wrinkled as a prune and set his back to the prisoners until dusk changed to night. Then he came to where they sat with arms tied behind them, squatted and said: 'It will not be much longer. For you this is pure luck. We will leave you behind, but alive.'

Lázaro's gaze did not leave the other man's face. 'It was my brother who was shot in the back not far from this place. Why?'

'I am sorry, but he was in the wrong place.'

'So he was shot just for being in the wrong place?'

'Yes. This will be finished in the next day or two.' Otero rose. 'After we are gone, you will be set afoot. By the time you walk to San Ildefonso, we will be too far away to be caught. You are very lucky. Your brother and the soldiers had no luck at all.'

Two youthful marauders spoon-fed the prisoners. They did not speak, and neither of them showed any expression. One of them had an old hogleg six-gun in the waist-band of his britches.

Lázaro knew marauders. These did not

appear to have a jug to pass around. Father Damion noticed and leaned to speak softly. 'The fair-skinned one, the *gachupín* ... show him the crucifix.'

Lázaro frowned. 'Why?'

'You have it?'

'Yes, in my pocket.'

'They will search us and find it. Before they do that, show it to the *gachupín*.' At Lázaro's continuing stubborn frown the priest whispered. 'They will take it anyway. Show it to him!'

Lázaro could not reach into his pocket nor could he imagine what the priest had in mind. He called quietly to the light-com-plected Mexican, who strolled over holding a tin cup of coffee. Lázaro told Otero, if he would untie one of his hands, he would show him something that might interest him.

Otero made no move to dig for his knife. 'You have a little gun?' he said.

Father Damion swore solemnly to God that Lázaro Guardia had no weapon.

Otero still did not lean forward. He looked steadily at Lázaro. 'Whatever it is, we will take it before we tie you for the night.'

Father Damion spoke sharply. 'If you don't see it now, you will never see it. Every man here is a thief. *Señor,* I give you my word. Untie one of his hands.'

Otero considered, drew his six-gun, cocked it, and held it in one hand as he told a nearby *mestizo* to untie the *alcalde*.

When this had been done, Otero lazily aimed his gun barrel from a distance of several feet at Lázaro's face and smiled. 'Be very prudent,' he said softly in Spanish.

Lázaro groped in a pocket, brought forth the old crucifix, and held it so that Joáquin Otero could see it. The *gachupín's* eyes widened. He did not move to take the crucifix. He said: 'Where did you get that?'

'From a dying *bandolero* who was where the six *gringo* soldiers were killed.'

Otero finally took the crucifix. Around the smokeless fire men neither moved nor spoke. The sweating man, who had cooked their meal, carefully put his pronged stick aside, wiped both hands, and said: 'He is alive, then, *Capitán*.'

Neither Lázaro nor the priest contradicted this statement, but Joáquin Otero raised black eyes to Lázaro's face and spoke quietly. 'A dying *bandolero?*'

'He had a name. John Smith.'

'He is alive?'

'No. He died. He had a very bad bullet wound. Everything that could be done for him, was done.'

'Did he give you this?'

'No. It was given to me by the man who hid the *bandolero* and tried to save his life. There was also fifteen dollars. He kept the money. I kept the crucifix.'

47

The short man built like a bull sidled up and gazed at the cross in Otero's hand. He breathed three words in Spanish. 'God be merciful.'

Otero let the crucifix slide out of his hand, walked away, off by himself, and sat among the jumble of saddles, blankets, bridles, *alforjas,* and casually leaning Winchesters.

Father Damion called to the man built like a bull who came over and hunkered. He looked at the priest as Father Damion said: 'It belonged to his brother. It came from the Convent of Sacred Angels near Hermasillo.'

The dark man made a humorless grin. 'He carried it for good fortune.'

Previously there had been conversation, even occasional laughter. Now there was total silence, and it lingered to the time the men went to their blankets.

Lázaro looked at the priest. 'How did you know that?'

Father Damion said simply: 'They are the only two men who look fair enough to be *gachupíns.* I wasn't hopeful, but they would have found it anyway.'

Lázaro Guardia, unlike his late brother, missed more Masses than he attended. He believed, but not in miracles, regardless of how earnestly Epifanio had tried to convince him otherwise. He muttered to the priest, who listened, said nothing, and lay back. It had been a long, arduous day.

Later, when someone snored like a pig caught under a gate, Joáquin Otero came silently to squat near Lázaro. 'Did he die hard?'

'Yes. He lingered mostly out of his head. They tried to hide him, but our local *curandero* told me where he was, and I went there.'

'He didn't give you the crucifix?'

'I told you, *señor*, no. The people who hid and cared for him had it. I took it from them to show to the priest.'

'He was too young. Ten years younger than I am. The young believe in overthrowing bad governments.'

'And you don't?'

'Not if I would have known this could happen. *Señor*, I am not a dreamer of heroic dreams.'

'So you will shoot me in the morning?'

Joáquin Otero rose and, as soundlessly as he had come, walked out into the darkness.

Chapter Four

Mother Of God!

East of San Ildefonso was the Jornada del Muerto – the Journey of the Dead Man. There was no water. The weather was capricious, usually very hot, but it could change with icy winds and drowning rain. There was the trickling Rio Salado that would have been a hot-water creek except for a more northerly watercourse called the Rio Puerco – Pig River. Where they joined, the water was salty. People and animals who drank salty water on the desert compounded their thirst, drank more, and died.

Once a great army up out of Mexico had traversed the Jornada del Muerto and had lost nearly all its animals, about half of its soldiers, many of the *soldaderas* who marched with Mexican armies – old mothers, wives, inamoratas – and also many children.

If *pronunciados* gathered at Juarez, south of the border, then camped along the Rio Grande, another piddling watercourse named as the old-time Spaniards seemed to name everything with a splendid designation, their route into the United States would be northward, the time-honored route of retreat for the defeated. San Ildefonso was north and west of the Journey of the Dead Man. Only part of it had to be crossed before San Ildefonso was reached through one of the passes, angling north-westerly through the San Mateo Mountains.

There were advantages and disadvantages. An advantage was that the youths Juan Bohorquez had sent to watch for dust coming up out of Mexico from high places along the San Mateos' spine could provide warnings. The disadvantage was obvious. A hamlet of less than a hundred and fifty souls would be at the mercy of defeated soldiers or commonplace marauders who usually came in considerable numbers and struck like a whirlwind.

Several of those mountain passes were deep with wide roadbeds. Traders from both sides of the border had taken caravans of wagons through those passes long before Mexico had lost the Southwest to *gringo* conquest. In earlier times war-like tribesmen had used those passes in their murderous raids, but with the advent of hordes of blue uniforms on large, strong horses brigandage had diminished.

At the Mexican camp, west of San Ildefonso, where Father Damion and Lázaro Guardia languished, a number of careless remarks plus the obvious fact that Captain

51

Otero's guerrillas showed clear signs in equal parts of restlessness and anticipation inclined Lázaro and the holy man to suspect that whatever the reason for the Mexicans to have a stationary camp the culmination was not too far off.

Joáquin Otero avoided the prisoners the day after the capture, but the following evening, with a blessed cool wind blowing, he brought over two tin cups of black Java. During the late afternoon most of the Mexicans had saddled up and ridden in a northeasterly direction. Otero sat down, sighed, and said: 'Give me the crucifix.'

Lázaro complied.

The tall, fair man sat, broodingly gazing at the crucifix before pocketing it and dryly saying: 'Superstition. Crucifixes, holy water, rituals, prayers ... superstition.'

Father Damion could not let those words pass. 'If you have no faith, *señor*, then all life is accidental, and God is a myth.'

Otero smiled, refused to be drawn into an argument, and asked Lázaro if those *gringo* soldiers he and his men had watched from hiding had said they would return.

Lázaro recalled no mention from Captain Bonham about the soldiers returning and said so.

Joáquin Otero gazed toward heat-hazed mountains. 'But they will. I have watchers. If they don't return by tomorrow...' Otero shrugged, rose, dusted off, and went over where two older Mexicans were lounging with backs supported by upturned saddles.

Father Damion softly said: 'They are waiting for something.'

Lázaro nodded while watching Otero and his companions.

'What will it be?' asked the priest.

His companion made a guess. 'Whatever revolutions need, Father.'

'Horses? Food supplies? Recruits from the north like Maria Alvarez's son?'

Lázaro turned and smiled slightly. 'Those things and more.'

A distant gunshot brought everyone in the camp upright and alert. Otero sent one old man to scout toward the east and another old marauder to scout toward the north.

Lázaro watched Otero and shook his head. 'He emptied the camp.'

Father Damion twisted as far as he could to scan the area. The gunshot had seemed to come from the east.

There was shade at the camp, and distant visibility was limited. Otero came toward the prisoners. He said: 'They will be looking for you.'

Lázaro gazed steadily at the *gachupín*. 'Maybe. Everyone knows by now there is danger in this part of the territory.'

Otero walked out a short distance, watching for movement. When he eventually saw it, he hunkered and waited. The horseman was sweat-stained. His horse showed signs of thirst. Otero told the man to loosen the *cincha* and water the animal. They walked together as the Mexican obeyed. They spoke earnestly. The marauder gestured often with his hands.

After the animal had been tanked up, the rider snugged up the *cincha*, mounted, swung, and rode back the way he had come. He was still in sight as Joáquin Otero approached the captives in their shade and abruptly stopped, stone still, staring south-westerly. Lázaro turned his head as did the holy man.

Two men, identically attired in blue uniforms, were slowly riding toward the camp. Lázaro recognized one even at a considerable distance. Captain Bonham.

Otero shot one swift look in the direction of his prisoners, then loosened his stance, and made a soundless sigh. Where Bonham drew rein was near the disorderly jumble of marauder equipment. Somewhere along the way he had yanked loose the flap of his regulation holster and tucked it so that the pistol's butt was exposed.

Even the prisoners did not have to know the soldier. It was written in his face, in the nearly lipless, tight-held mouth, in the steady gaze of his sunken eyes, and in the set of his jaw – Frank Bonham did not compromise.

He gestured with his gloves in the direction of Lázaro and the priest. 'Set them loose, mister.' When Otero did not move, Bonham jerked his head and the soldier who had accompanied him moved to free the prisoners. Captain Bonham considered the camp, the disarray, the equipment, and brought his gaze back to Joáquin Otero. 'You are in charge?'

'Yes. Joáquin Otero.'

'What are you doing here?'

Otero remained silent, so Father Damion said: 'They are waiting for something. Whatever it is, it is supposed to arrive today or tomorrow.'

Captain Bonham folded the gloves over and under his garrison belt – and smiled. '*Señor*, what are you waiting for?'

Otero neither spoke nor looked away from Bonham. The captain growled something to his companion who mounted and loped back the way they had come. Captain Bonham said: 'Shed that pistol.' After he had been obeyed, he said: '*Señor*, the cargo will not come out here.'

Otero's jaw muscles rippled, but he remained silent.

Bonham considered the freed prisoners and addressed Lázaro. 'Find your weapons, anything else you want, take it.' He returned his attention to the tall Mexican. 'You have a rank?'

'*Capitán.*'

Bonham nodded. 'That's my rank too. Captain, I have a little story to tell you. Would you like to hear it?'

'Very much, but I don't know your name.'

'Frank Bonham. Would you care to move into the shade and sit down?'

Bonham followed Otero into shade but did not sit as Otero did. He produced a plug of Kentucky twist, offered it, got back a negative shake of the head, worried off a corner, pouched it into his cheek and turned aside to expectorate. When he faced forward, he said: 'Did you hear a gunshot an hour or so earlier?'

'Yes.'

'There was a thick-set, very dark man coming toward San Ildefonso. He saw my vidette, yanked around, and would have run like the wind. He was shot out of the saddle. I thought maybe the horse would come back here. Have you seen it?'

'No. Why did you have him shot?'

'When I returned to Fort Sedgewick and reported, the commanding colonel ordered me to return with a full company of horse. We were settling in San Ildefonso when the Mexican saw us an' tried to run. Captain, I had a long talk with the man who owns the general store. Does that mean anything to you?'

Otero did not reply.

Bonham shifted his cud before speaking again. 'You ever hear of a big wholesaler in Santa Fé named Bannerman?'

'No.'

'I'll tell you what happened, Captain. Moses Morisco placed a pretty big order and paid cash in advance. Bannerman had to dig a little to fill the order, but he filled it an' hired a freighter named Flaherty to deliver the load to Morisco in San Ildefonso. You know what I'm talking about? No? Well, maybe you don't know that much, but you sure as hell know the rest.

'Flaherty was stopped by Mexicans and given a piece of paper written in English. Flaherty was not to go the full distance to San Ildefonso. He was to leave the road an' follow the Mexicans. He didn't do it, Captain. Before he left Santa Fé, he sent a wireless to Fort Sedgewick. That's why I was given a full company, an' they're what we surrounded Flaherty's wagon an' the Mexicans with. We got the Mexicans locked in a house in San Ildefonso under twenty-four hour guard. The same as will happen to you an' the others you camped out here with.'

Captain Bonham turned discreetly to expectorate, faced back, and added: 'You know what Flaherty was hauling, Captain Otero? Cat's got your tongue again, eh? His wagon was loaded with twenty-six wooden rifle crates and eleven crates of rifle ammunition.

Can you imagine that, Mister Otero? All that firepower to be delivered at a general store in a town that doesn't have half enough people if them guns was handed out.'

A full company of dragoons was approaching from the southwest. They cleared the last strands of flourishing underbrush and closed ranks, riding at a walk.

Captain Bonham ignored them. 'Captain Otero, from what I know about Mexican *pronunciados,* they'd shoot you for losing them guns and ammunition. If you want to stay alive, you'd better never go back down there. I expect we got as many of your *compañeros* as we need.'

For the first time Joáquin Otero spoke. 'If you have the men I sent to lead the wagon out here, that leaves two old men out scouting who have by now seen your soldiers and will be impossible to find.'

'That's all?'

Otero shrugged. 'No. I sent one to Juarez to say we would have the wagon today and would start back.'

Captain Bonham raised his eyes to Lázaro and the priest. They nodded. He jettisoned his cud, spat, and returned his attention to the *gachupín.* 'I'm sorry about your brother.'

Lázaro and Father Damion stared, but the officer offered no explanation of how he knew about the younger *gachupín* who had used a *gringo* name.

58

Bonham had horses saddled. He placed Joáquin Otero in the middle of his dragoons and, except for making sure he had no hide-out weapon, made no further attempt to restrict his prisoner.

They might have reached San Ildefonso before sundown, except that the captain sashayed northeasterly until he found the place where the freight wagon had been stopped. He studied the sign for several minutes, then led off to the roadway, and turned southward.

The sun was almost gone when the cavalcade rode into San Ildefonso where, unlike more northerly *gringo* towns where everyone turned out to see soldiers, bringing in a prisoner, the residents of San Ildefonso remained discreetly inside. Bodies of armed men had passed through before. People had ignored them and did so this time.

Lázaro had help caring for the animals. Generally the troopers had little to say. After Captain Bonham led Joáquin Otero away, one red-headed dragoon, wearing sergeant's chevrons, let go a long sigh and led the exodus in the direction of Juan Bohorquez's saloon.

Father Damion lingered in the corral yard. He told Lázaro it would not surprise him if the hard-eyed officer with a wound for a mouth did not hold a hanging at sunrise, and, at the look he got from Lázaro, the priest shrugged and started walking as he said: 'I don't think they are much different.'

San Ildefonso, where candles cost money, traditionally retired after supper, which was about eight or nine o'clock. This night was little different, but for the company of blue uniforms who kept lights burning in several buildings. Some formed quartets and sang, not uncommonly about their forlorn and destitute homeland over the seas – Ireland.

Captain Bonham came searching for Lázaro Guardia at the way station. He had been drinking, but it showed only in his desire for someone to talk to other than his dragoons.

During the course of their conversation the captain made one remark that lingered in Lázaro's mind. Bonham said: 'It don't really make much difference whether they get them guns or not. If they had 'em, they'd thin out the ranks of the troublesome sons-of-bitches who come stormin' up here.'

Lázaro's retort was short. 'But your Army does not let weapons go down there, does it?'

'No. But if it comes to it, we try to prevent trouble for the sake of peace in places like San Ildefonso that are on our side of the line.' The captain smiled without a shred of humor. 'I'd a damned sight rather chase Indians and renegades. Mister Guardia, I'm obliged for your help.'

Lázaro studied the hard-eyed *gringo*. 'All the holy man and I did was ride into an ambush and get caught.'

Captain Bonham nodded and left.

Lázaro was tired to the bone. He bedded down on the cot in the back of the room and did not awaken until old Maria Alvarez's damned rooster, that had a voice like a foghorn, awakened him. The sun was bringing new-day brilliance to the desert. He washed out back at the trough, did the chores his brother had formerly done, and went after something to eat.

San Ildefonso's eatery was a hole in the wall north of Morisco's general store. Its proprietor was a fat man named Fulgencio Aramas. He was by nature a recluse who lived in a lean-to behind the café. He rarely spoke, and his black forelock was no more than four inches above his eyes. He watched Lázaro sit down and, after some delay, brought a thick crockery plate with refried beans, some kind of spiced meat, and half of a sliced apple. His coffee was known far and wide as a black fluid upon which a horseshoe could be floated.

He retired to his cooking area and remained there, emerging only when he heard the roadway door close. Lázaro had a suspicion that Fulgencio Aramas had been a marauder, an opinion he shared with others who saw in the beetle-browed, dark, heavy man the common conception of a brigand.

Moses Morisco met Lázaro outside his store. He seemed to Lázaro to be distinctly uncomfortable, but, when they briefly exchanged greetings, the storekeeper said nothing to support Lázaro's suspicion. If Morisco had talked, Lázaro would have responded instantly.

He walked out to his brother's grave where someone had left a bouquet of wild flowers.

San Ildefonso was beginning to return to its normal lassitude. Torres Mendoza was talking to several men out front of the *cantina*. Lázaro could guess the subject. Torres had been impressed during his brief stay below the border. This time, the uprising would succeed. It had as leaders professional soldiers. From what he knew of contraband weaponry reaching Mexico, Lázaro felt less sanguine than he had felt about other revolutions.

His greatest shock came when he met Juan Bohorquez near the north end of the village. Juan Bohorquez looked long at Lázaro before taking him by the arm and leading him through a dogtrot on the west side of the street into a crooked, dusty and empty alleyway. There he released the arm and said: 'The soldiers will leave today.'

Lázaro shrugged. Soldiers never stayed long.

'And the wagon has already departed ...

driven by two of the *prisoneros*. The other prisoners went as outriders.'

Lázaro stared in dumb silence.

'They left about sunup this morning.'

'Are you crazy? The *gringo* captain had them locked up and guarded.'

Bohorquez made a cruel small smile. 'It is the truth. He used his soldiers to put them on the wagon and on horses around it. Right now, the soldiers are striking their camp to leave.'

Lázaro reddened. 'What kind of foolishness are you saying?'

'Go see for yourself. The soldiers will leave soon, and the wagon and its marauders are already gone. It was parked by Moses Morisco's store. Go talk to the Jew. He had to know.'

Lázaro considered the burly man whose countenance was strained and whose gaze did not leave Lázaro's face. Eventually Guardia remembered Bonham's remarks the night before. He didn't care if the *pronunciados* got the guns and ammunition. It would mean fewer raiders, coming across the line, if the *Federales* beat the revolutionaries. Even if they didn't beat them, if the revolutionaries whipped the federal soldiers, there was a good chance that in their drunken sense of triumph they would come boiling up over the border to murder, burn, and pillage. It had happened before many times.

He left Juan Bohorquez in the alley, went hurriedly back to the general store, waited until Morisco had finished with two elderly women, carrying knit shopping bags. The moment they were alone, he asked about the wagon. Moses Morisco paled and shifted his stance behind the counter where his money drawer was located.

Lázaro reached across the counter. *'Tell me!'*

Instead of replying, the storekeeper jerked his head, led the way to his loading dock out back, down its four steps, and across the alley to a dilapidated storage shed. Before opening the door, Morisco looked in every direction, then yanked one door open, and moved aside.

Lázaro stepped inside. It was a dark, musty-smelling place. Morisco cut off what light there was by closing the door after himself. He groped along one wall and told Lázaro to do the same. What Lázaro's hand came into contact with was stacked rifles, dozens of them, most with the manufacturer's light oil on the working parts.

Morisco turned back, wordlessly opened the door, closed it after Lázaro, and wordlessly reëntered his store. It was empty and cool. He said: 'They worked most of the night.'

'Why?' Lázaro asked.

Morisco made a fluttery gesture with both

hands before speaking. 'Why? Why would you think? They refilled the crates with rocks and paper. Nailed them closed and the officer brought his prisoners. I heard him tell them in Spanish they were free to go, and they must not stop until they are over the border. The last thing he said to them was that the revolutionaries would repay them greatly.' Morisco paused, watching Lázaro's face before speaking again. 'You understand? They will arrive down there as proud as peacocks, expecting to be treated as heroes of the uprising, until the crates are opened, then they will be lined up and shot.'

Lázaro left the store to stand briefly under its roadway overhang before going in search of the captain and his soldiers.

At the north end of the village Maria Alvarez was standing with one hand shielding her eyes and cackling with laughter. She raised her other hand to gesture with. Lázaro squinted into the distance. He could make out the blue uniforms as a mass. He could see the little swallow-tailed guidon out front.

Maria said: 'I was young when they came before, dragging cannons and with many wagons. That time they planted their *gringo* flag in the plaza. Ordered everyone to line up and searched for weapons, which they took away with them. This time...' She cackled again. 'This time they caught some *bandoleros*. Maybe they took them with them. If they did, they'll only go until they find trees and hang them.'

Lázaro considered chasing after Captain Bonham. He was still considering this when Efraim Montoya came up, squinting as always, and said: 'Do you know what they did?'

Lázaro nodded.

'Do you know why they did it?'

This time Lázaro frowned irritably as he replied: 'To get the men with the wagon shot when it is discovered in Juarez there are rocks instead of rifles in those boxes.'

The *curandero* smiled. 'You are young, Lázaro. You aren't even a good Mexican. You are more of a *gringo.*'

'What are you talking about, *viejo?*'

Montoya slowly turned his squinty gaze to Lázaro. 'The *gringos* learned how it is in this countryside. For a long time they didn't learn, but now they have. That *capitán* replaced the rifles with rocks. Such a thing will enrage the revolutionaries. They will shoot the men who brought them crates of rocks ... but ... who put the rocks in there? They will come up out of *Méjico* for revenge. Maybe an army of them this time. What was done to them was done here in San Ildefonso. Now do you comprehend?'

Lázaro ignored Maria's demented cackling. He stared at Efraim Montoya so long the old man had to ease his weight on the

66

least troublesome of his legs as he stared back, but, as the silence continued, Efraim made a snort of disgust and walked away.

Lázaro returned southward. Juan Bohorquez hailed him from the saloon doorway. Lázaro might not have heard. He went the full distance to his small adobe way station office, sank down at the table he used for a desk, and said: *'Madre de Dios.'*

He was still sitting there a half hour later when Francesca Cardinál appeared in the doorway. She stepped inside where it was cool and said: 'They are gone, those soldiers, and so is the freight wagon. Its owner came banging on my door for a place to stay until he can round up riders to go after those who stole his wagon and mules. I told him to see you. Did he come here? He is very angry.'

Chapter Five

The Inexperienced

Lázaro went to the *cantina*. Juan Bohorquez drew off a small glass of wine, thick with sediment, and drew off one for himself. He cocked his head at Lázaro. 'The captain is a shrewd man. When they open the boxes, they will shoot the *guerrilleros.*' Bohorquez shrugged. 'That many fewer.'

Lázaro emptied the glass and pushed it aside. 'Do you still have those watchers on the topouts?'

'No. What for? The soldiers are gone, and the others will never come back. They will bury them down there.'

'Juan, if there is a big army down there...'

'It *is* big. My cousin told me the whole countryside is rising.'

As though there had been no interruption, Lázaro went on: 'Those rocks were put in the rifle crates here. In San Ildefonso. That's where the *gachupín's* men were freed to out-ride the wagon. There will be watchers on the border. They will send word that the wagon is coming.'

'I know all this,' the saloonman said.

'Do you know what those men down there will do after they shoot the men with the wagon? They will come here for revenge. It is bad enough they have been made fools of by that soldier. It is worse that it was done in San Ildefonso.'

Bohorquez refilled the glasses and downed his drink in one swallow. He refilled his glass again but did not touch it. He pushed the bottle aside and leaned on his counter. 'We had nothing to do with it.'

Lázaro threw up his hands in disgust. 'Do you think that will mean anything to the revolutionaries? What Captain Bonham did was make those angry men down below want to wipe out this village. Maybe he didn't think it through, or maybe he did, but it doesn't matter. Do you comprehend?'

Bohorquez understood.

Lázaro told the saloonman, if it was possible, he should keep those youthful horsemen in high places so that they could warn of dust, any kind of sign Mexicans were crossing the border. Bohorquez agreed. The last thing he said as Lázaro was leaving was: 'We should light the bonfires.'

Lázaro shook his head negatively as he was passing through the doors. They had to be sure invaders were coming before lighting the fires.

An unexpected stage arrived from the north. The driver went to the saloon where he learned of San Ildefonso's problem. He promised to carry the message back up north and to see that the Santa Fé garrison was informed.

It was a good gesture, but Lázaro knew better than others that the stage stopped at several villages before reaching Santa Fé. Whatever happened would probably have already happened before the coach could provide possible aid. As for the Army, it did not move swiftly unless its own people were attacked. Its customary attitude toward small villages such as San Ildefonso was to order patrols to go out of their way to ascertain the validity of rumors, which meant a lightning attack on the village would be over and finished with before a patrol happened along, and, because routine border patrols usually consisted of one or two squads of riders, their numbers would be insufficient to make a difference in the outcome of an attack.

Lázaro went to see Isabel Montenegro. He knew the mustangers had left a week or more ago. They were the young men of San Ildefonso. Isabel told him he could not rely on her husband because José knew of no way to find the young men. Isabel's husband was a drunkard. To consider him as a member of the local defense was demoralizing. Lázaro talked with everyone about forming a defense. Many of the people had heard the full story and were preparing to leave. A defense against a guerrilla army was hopeless.

He spent two days going among the out-
lying ranches and other hamlets. What he
accomplished was to frighten the people,
and, although some men spoke loudly of
fighting, Lázaro's impression was that these
men did this to impress their families and
neighbors. When the flight began, they
would be among those who would flee.

The evening of the second day he called a
meeting in the *cantina*. Mostly those who
came were old. They had fought off other
attacks and were adamant about doing the
same this time. Their women were grimly
silent and bitter.

Juan Bohorquez said afterwards he had
counted those willing to fight.

Lázaro asked how many.

Juan dryly replied: 'Eighteen men and half
that many women. How many *guerrilleros*
will there be?'

Lázaro had no idea, but, if it had been a
large band, waiting to be armed down in
Juarez, it could be five times eighteen, and
possibly more.

Juan recalled something his father had told
him. There was a bronze cannon in one of the
monk cells below the church. Lázaro had
heard this story without placing much faith
in it. 'Have you seen this gun?' he asked.

Bohorquez hadn't, but it was unthinkable
that Father Damion wouldn't know. Lázaro

went to the mission. Father Damion was not there. An old white-headed man said the priest was giving last rites to an ancient *mestiza* named Dolores Santa Cruz. Lázaro went to the Santa Cruz hovel, met Father Damion leaving, and asked about the cannon. The priest remembered being told of such a thing by his predecessor. They returned to the mission, descended to the dark, musty series of small cells where in better days resident monks had lived, and found the cannon.

It was very old, massive, and was mounted on a steel-reinforced sled. Beneath the dust of many years was inscribed in Spanish – Fourth Ligero Regiment, Vera Cruz – and a date, 1826. Father Damion pondered aloud how the gun had been brought down to the monk's cell. Lázaro was wondering how they could get it up out of there. Two men could not lift even one corner.

Lázaro asked if the priest would get men of the village to help.

Father Damion agreed but asked: 'Is there powder and balls? It will be useless to do all the straining, getting it up from here, if it cannot be fired.'

Lázaro patted the priest's shoulder as he turned toward the door. 'If you can get it out of here, I'll find what we'll need to shoot it.'

After Lázaro departed, the priest gazed dispassionately at the gun. *Why had it been hidden where it was, and who had got it down here?*

He would never have answers. Whoever had hidden the gun had by now been dead at least two generations, maybe more like three or four.

Lázaro met Moses Morisco out front of the general store. The merchant said he and several others had brought all those rifles from his shed inside the store. They were being wiped clean of grease and tested for firing. He also said he had emptied his shelves of bullets for the rifles. What he wanted to know in particular was to whom he should give guns and bullets and dryly said: 'If we had a man for every gun, we could put up a formidable defense, but we lack half that number, and most are as old as I am.'

San Ildefonso was alive with activity. Only Isabel Montenegro was unconvinced there would be an attack. Her reason was that she had heard through the *huaracha* grapevine that there had already been a battle in Chihuahua Province, somewhere between Guzman and Santa Maria, where the revolutionaries had ambushed a federal route army and had not only defeated it, but fleeing *Federales* were stripping the province of horses on which to escape.

Lázaro asked one question. 'Which way did they flee, north or south?'

Isabel did not know, only that Chihuahua was in turmoil. Lázaro carried this information to everyone he met and added his notion that, if fleeing *Federales* were seeking asylum over the border in the United States, they might reach San Ildefonso in less than two or three days. Efraim Montoya, wearing a shell belt and ancient dragoon pistol with a barrel half as long as his withered forearm, thought it possible that scattering bands of Mexico's soldiers might not come near San Ildefonso, but, if they did and their numbers were not great, the defenders could handle them.

To this Francesca Cardinál's husband, Rafael, a man who rarely smiled and who detested *norteamericanos,* said: 'If ... Efraim ... *if* they do this or that, we should know.'

Juan Bohorquez loudly said he would send some of his youths southward, which quieted Rafael Cardinál, although his facial expression showed unrequited misgivings.

Isabel Montenegro's story was not the only one that circulated. It appeared that over half of the people had ideas which they spread. To Lázaro Guardia a new problem arose. He heard the wildest rumors and wasted time scoffing at them. If Isabel Montenegro's story was true, Lázaro felt certain San Ildefonso would be attacked soon, perhaps as early as the following day or evening.

A perspiring Father Damion Sanchez sought Lázaro to say they had got the cannon up out of its cell and had pulled it on its steel runners to the south end of the village where it was out of sight and pointing southward. His concern was what to fire it with.

They went to Moses Morisco, whose store resembled an armory. Men, even women, were cleaning rifles, dry firing them, and counting out bullets. Moses listened and said: 'I keep six barrels of blasting powder in the stone house behind my shed. It doesn't sell well, only to fools who think they can mine gold and others who have to move boulders or deepen wells, most of which collapse when dynamite goes off down in the holes.' Moses asked a simple question. 'Do you know how to fire a cannon?'

Neither Lázaro nor the priest had any idea about firing a cannon.

Moses said: 'Maria Alvarez's husband used dynamite many times, searching for water.'

Father Damion wagged his head. 'He has been dead ten years.'

'I know,' Moses replied. 'But he took Maria with him many times.'

The three men looked at one another before Moses spoke again.

'She saw how he did it.'

Father Damion told them he would go talk to Maria Alvarez. The way he spoke made it clear he was not hopeful.

Moses had an idea. 'How many cannon balls are there?'

'None,' Lázaro said, and the storekeeper offered his solution. 'I have seven kegs of nails, and behind the smithy there is a large mound of old shoes for horses and oxen.'

Lázaro left the store, beginning to feel more confident. He went to the *cantina* where Juan Bohorquez had just spoken to one of his youthful spies. There were several dust banners coming north. Two of them split wide and would in all probability bypass San Ildefonso. When he paused, Lázaro said: 'And the others?'

'Coming this way. Two bands. From the dust the spy said it might be forty to sixty riders.'

'How long before they get here?'

Juan spread his hands palms down. 'The boy guessed maybe tonight or in the morning.'

Lázaro was leaving the saloon when he said: 'Tell the spies to keep a close watch.'

He searched for the priest and found him, coming south from Maria Alvarez's *jacal*.

Father Damion said: 'She remembers. She fired some charges for her husband. But...'

'But what?'

'She is very excited, waves her arms, and talks very fast. I think she likes the idea of San Ildefonso being attacked.'

'Will she fire the gun?'

'She said she would. She has a coil of the primer used for shooting cannons. Lázaro, she won't be reliable. She's crazier than usual. She told me her son, the horse hunter,

76

visited day before yesterday, and she told him *guerrilleros* are going to attack the village.'

'And?'

'That is all. Her son left to rejoin the other horse hunters. Lázaro, she has been saying attackers are coming for years. Why should we believe her now?'

Efraim Montoya found Lázaro Guardia in the way station corral yard. He looked more elfin and grotesque than usual with that big old horse pistol, dragging his britches down on one side. He said: 'Isabel Montenegro hasn't spoken to her son, Leonides, since he married that Indian girl.'

Lázaro nodded impatiently. This was not new information. Everyone in San Ildefonso knew Isabel had disowned her son.

Efraim continued. 'The *indio* is going to have a child. I told Isabel to go help her. She almost spat in my face.'

'Why don't you help the girl?'

'Because I keep watch from the *cantina's* roof. It is the highest building.' Efraim hesitated. 'She is young. This is her first child. I examined her last month. I don't see how she can make a delivery without help. You know about foaling mares...'

Lázaro heard men calling back and forth northward and across the roadway. 'Tell Juan to put someone else on the roof.'

'I went to tell him. The *cantina* is closed and

77

locked. Juan is out at the dynamite house, helping load. The cannon must be fed. You could get on the roof.'

A sweating youth on a sweating horse loped past. Lázaro said – 'Someone else must go up there!' – and hurried to find the rider, who had stopped to tie up in front of the saloon. They knew each other well.

The boy said: 'Dust from riders. They are coming, and we can see the men on their horses. Maybe an hour they will be here.'

Lázaro took the horse's reins. 'Get up on the saloon roof where Efraim has been watching. Yell when they are closer.'

He led the winded animal to his corral yard, dumping its saddle and bridle. Under the puzzled gaze of the *curandero*, who had remained behind, he led the horse to drink, sparingly, then put it in a stall where hot sunlight would not blister the salt sweat on its back. When he faced around, Efraim said: 'What is it?'

'They are coming. The boy saw them.'

'How many?'

'I don't know. Go help the Indian girl.'

Efraim moved fast as far as the road, where he halted to peer southward. Lázaro called to him. 'They aren't *that* close. Go care for the woman!'

The hard-ridden horse dropped down to roll over. Then it stood up, wide-legged, and shook all over. Lázaro leaned on the stall door and turned when a man he knew only by sight, a goat rancher who sold milk in San Ildefonso, approached and said: 'My name is Alfredo Lopez. I have goats three miles west of San Ildefonso. Last night many horsemen went by. When my dog ran out to bark, one of them stopped and shot my dog.' Alfredo Lopez was a tall, dark, thin man. In age he could have been somewhere between forty and sixty. 'I was on the porch because I heard riders. When the man shot my dog, I shot the man.' Lopez handed Lázaro a Colt revolver with a Mexican eagle carved on both grips. 'You can see the man. I dragged him into a goat shed. He was a *Federale* in uniform.'

Lázaro examined the six-gun. Whoever the carver had been, he was very good. Lázaro handed the gun back and said: 'I'll loan you a mule to bring the dead man to town.'

Lopez nodded. 'It will take time. First, I have to bury my dog. I am unmarried and have no children. That dog was like a child to me.'

'Which way were the horsemen riding?'

'Northwest toward Chinle.'

'Can you guess how many?'

'No, *señor*, except that from the sound I would guess maybe twenty or thirty. I thought they would come back after two gunshots but they didn't. *Señor*, if you wish, I will light the warning fire. It is not very far from my house. Chinle should be warned.'

Lázaro nodded. The village of Chinle, no larger than San Ildefonso, was roughly fifteen miles northwest. 'Light the fire,' he told the tall man. 'Care for your dog, then bring me the dead *Federale*.'

'Why would Mexican federal soldiers be up here?' Lopez asked.

Lázaro had no idea, unless they were in pursuit of enemies. By treaty between Mexico and the United States soldiers of neither country were to cross into the country of the other. Lopez said: 'They weren't chasing anyone. I would have heard it, if they had been.'

Lázaro went after a stout nine-hundred-pound mule, put a pack rig on it, and handed the shank to Alfred Lopez.

The tall man said nothing as he walked away, leading the mule.

Isabel Montenegro appeared. She had watched the tall man, departing with the mule, but did not mention that. She told Lázaro the *curandero* had told her the Indian her son had chosen to marry against her wishes was going to give birth. Lázaro nodded. 'It is true,' he said. 'Efraim is going to be there.'

Isabel spat her next words. 'That unwashed disposer of his failures!'

'You wouldn't help.'

'Well ... I *will* help. I know what it is to give birth.'

'Why aren't you with your girl, then? Why

are you telling me this?'

'Because Maria Alvarez told me you have a cannon but don't know how to fire it. My husband can shoot a cannon. He did it down in Mexico years ago.'

'Is he sober?'

Isabel Montenegro drew herself stiffly to her full height. 'José suffers agonies from a ruined back. Nothing stops the pain. He uses *pulque* for relief from the pain. He is sober.'

Lázaro smiled apologetically. 'We need him to fire the cannon.'

As Isabel Montenegro turned, she said brusquely: 'I will send him to you, but first I will see the *indio!*'

Despite Isabel's promise José Montenegro did not appear, but Lázaro's disappointment was brief. Juan Bohorquez came to the corral yard. He and others had brought gunpowder from the stone house east of Morisco's store. What they needed now was someone who knew how much powder to put into the cannon and also to help fill it with whatever could be found, preferably pieces of steel rather than rocks.

Lázaro crossed the road with the burly saloonman and was about to pass between two buildings to the east-side alley when Father Damion hailed them.

'Maria won't leave her house,' he called. 'She bit my hand and tried to claw my face.'

Lázaro nodded. 'Go get José Montenegro.

He has fired cannons.'

The priest looked skeptical but went hurriedly in the direction of the Montenegro residence.

Juan Bohorquez led the way and spoke over his shoulder as he did so. 'He will blow us all up. Why did you send for him?'

'Because Isabel said he fired cannons down in Mexico.'

Bohorquez snorted. 'He probably blew up whoever was foolish enough to be close by. Besides, he will be drunk. Lázaro, someone should see if Morisco has got the rifles ready.'

Lázaro did not respond. There was a small crowd of people, mostly men but also some women, hovering around the stubby but formidable-looking cannon on its sled. Kegs of powder were near the back wall of the nearest building. Men were standing by with old, rusted horseshoes and oxenshoes in a pile. Other townsmen had the last of the bullets from Morisco's store.

Juan Bohorquez asked if he should assist Father Damion in getting Isabel's husband. Lázaro preferred to keep the saloonman with him. Instead, he sent Torres Mendoza who was less likely to try to beat Isabel's husband into sobriety. The fat caféman, Fulgencio Aramas, was shaking his head. No one had to ask why he was doing that – there had never been as disorganized and ill-prepared a band of defenders! The fat man ruefully smiled. 'If

82

God allows a miracle...! Otherwise...?' The caféman had just spoken more words than anyone had heard him say in months.

Chapter Six

The Long Night

Father Damion gathered all the people he could find and led them to the old mission church. Lázaro was there but too worried to pay attention to the priest, now waving incense, speaking prayers in Latin, and asking for divine intercession while kneeling below the magnificent carving of the crucified Christ whose expression of agony and resignation had been perfectly realized in the carving.

Lázaro was seated near the rear. Beside him was the white-headed, very dark, and wrinkled Tomás Henriques. His lips moved in silence. His eyes were closed. When Lázaro moved, the old man opened his eyes and looked around. He whispered to Lázaro. 'I am *penitente*. I ask for forgiveness for stealing horses and cattle, for shooting men, for many bad things.'

Lázaro nodded, twisted to look past the open doors, and the old man tugged at his sleeve.

'*Yo sé el asilo donde un secreto era escondido.*'

Lázaro gazed at the old man. He knew him

84

only by sight as someone who attended to the mission, serving without pay for the benefit of his soul. Father Damion allowed the old man to live in one of the many tiny rooms. After what the old man said, he had Lázaro's full interest. There was scarcely an old mission that did not have secrets, ancient rumors, stories, at times gruesome. He had heard a number of those old tales while growing up. His brother had been inclined to credit them. Lázaro was not, and never had been, a believer, but, as Father Damion prayed below the effigy, Lázaro asked the old man what secret he was talking about.

The old man pinched his black eyes nearly closed and leaned to whisper. 'Where the holy treasure is. Jesus told me.'

Lázaro leaned slightly away from the old man. Father Damion had finished the service. As he passed Lázaro and the old man in the aisle on his way to stand beside the door while people departed, he rolled his eyes.

Once the church emptied, Torres Mendoza asked Father Damion to come and bless the little cannon. He and the priest departed side by side. Behind them the sun was reddening in the west. A very faint scent of burning wood rode the still air.

When Lázaro reached his corral yard, Alfredo Lopez was waiting with the big mule, both apparently exhibiting immense patience. Lázaro helped the goat man lift down the dead Mexican soldier and carry him where there was shade. Lázaro then cared for the mule before taking Alfredo Lopez to his office where they both had a glass of tawny-colored wine. Afterward they returned to the corpse.

Either the goat man was an incredibly good shot, or he'd been blessed with uncommon good fortune. He had fired at the soldier from his porch in the dark. The *Federale* hadn't known what had hit him. He was dead before he hit the ground. He was not a young man, and from the appearance of his uniform, which was faded and soiled, he was a regular, not an *activo*, member of Mexico's militia. He was armed with a knife with a wicked blade and a very small under-and-over pistol with a three-inch barrel. His pockets yielded a cornucopia of gold coins, about half of which were of U.S. origin.

What Lázaro learned from the corpse was only what was obvious. Mexican soldiers in uniform had invaded the United States. Why had they done this and in what numbers, Lázaro could only guess. He gave the goat man a silver coin to take the corpse somewhere and bury it. Everything Lázaro had gleaned from the soldier's pockets he put into the man's bandanna and kept. Alfredo Lopez said he would need the mule to take the corpse away. Lázaro brought forth the animal, helped tie the dead man on, and, as before, handed the goat man the lead rope.

He was in the corral yard office, sorting through the items from the bandanna, when Efraim Montoya entered, stared at what was lying atop the bandanna, and puffed out his cheeks. Lázaro swept the bandanna and its contents into a drawer and scowled at the *curandero*. 'You delivered the baby?' he asked.

Montoya went to a bench to sit before answering. 'A boy. Did you know when Indians are born, they have a full head of hair?'

'How is the woman?'

'She could be up and at work tomorrow. That's how her people do it. Did you send Isabel Montenegro up there?'

'I didn't send her. She told me she was going. Why?'

'She wanted me to leave.'

'Did you?'

'Certainly. The baby was in his grandmother's arms. There was no reason for me to stay. I told her I was surprised that she had blood in her veins and a heart in her chest.' Montoya narrowed his eyes in a shrewd stare. 'That is done. Did you know San Ildefonso is surrounded?'

Lázaro rose. '*You* know this?'

'Yes. One of the boys who spies for Juan Bohorquez came in a small while ago and said he had heard it. Juan Bohorquez is going to see if it is true.'

Lázaro sighed. 'If it is true, he could get himself killed.'

Efraim grinned widely. 'I don't think so. He took with him the fat caféman who was for many years a *guerrillero*. He knows about ambushes.' Efraim got up, flexed one leg, and went to the door to gaze up and down the roadway before he spoke without turning. 'Do you know old Tomás Henriques who lives at the mission?'

'I know him. I sat next to him in church. White-headed.'

'*Sí*. Tomás Henriques.' Montoya faced around, wearing a humorless smile. 'He says we will beat the border jumpers. He told me it will be a bloody fight, but that no matter how we are outnumbered, we will win. Do you know why?'

'Why?'

'Because he called upon Jesus to come, and Jesus told the old man that he would come.' Efraim's black eyes were sardonic. 'I have to get back atop the *cantina*. If I see them out there ... it will be dark soon. *Adiós*.'

Lázaro went across to the store. Moses Morisco was asleep in a cubbyhole office. Lázaro spoke to some of the people who had worked with the new rifles. They had been told by Juan Bohorquez to pass the guns around with as much ammunition as was left to be divided.

88

Father Damion met Lázaro in front of the store with dusk approaching to say the cannon was loaded and primed, and that – miracles of miracles – José Montenegro was sober. Shaky but stone sober.

Lázaro asked the priest if he had heard San Ildefonso was surrounded, and Father Damion made a humorless smile. 'I can tell you who started that story. Maria Alvarez. She went among the people wild-eyed. Did you see her?'

'No. The *curandero* told me.'

Father Damion made a grimace. 'He is as bad as she is. He is happiest when he can upset people.'

'He also said Juan and some others went out to see.'

Father Damion wagged his head. 'Juan is with the cannon where he has been since midday. Some day someone will cut out the tongue of that old bag of bones.'

Lázaro was of the opinion there should be watchers sent out on all sides of the village. It was not impossible, he told the priest, that San Ildefonso was surrounded. He also told him about the dead *Federale*.

Father Damion's eyebrows crept upwards like caterpillars. 'Alfredo Lopez?'

'Yes. I loaned him a mule to take the dead man away and bury him.'

'Alfredo Lopez was raised among Indians. He has never entered the mission.'

Lázaro shrugged. 'He is a very good shot, Father. When he brings my mule back, I'll ask him to stay.'

The holy man understood. His private disapproval of Alfredo Lopez did not extend to Lázaro Guardia. He said: 'I'll find some men and scout beyond the village.'

'Be careful, Father.'

The priest made a genuine smile and walked away.

It would be a long night, rumors would fly, people would pray and make certain their weapons were in firing condition. One of Juan Bohorquez's horseback youths returned shortly before sunset. What he had to say put Maria Alvarez's frightening tale to sleep. The youth reported that the *guerrilleros* had gone into camp several miles from San Ildefonso. He also said that someone had set the warning mound of dry faggots afire, that it could be seen for miles, and that after dark it would be even more visible. What he did not mention, and what troubled Lázaro Guardia, was that Mexican regular troops had been seen and identified.

When he went to join the people with the little cannon and mentioned his worry to the saloonman, Bohorquez wondered if the battle which evidently the federal army had lost might not have resulted in chaos and murder on a large scale. There would be no prisoners taken. Throughout the southwest border country it was common knowledge that, whichever side won, the mindless savagery was worse than anything Indians had ever done.

Juan Bohorquez's youthful watchers all returned to the village before dusk. They said the invaders had strong scouting parties out in three directions. If the youths had lingered, they would have been flanked and captured.

This night candles would burn, and few would sleep. The women did what they did best under these circumstances. They cooked mounds of tortillas, *entomotados*, and pots of hot beans. They also brought pitchers of *cerveza* and allowed only one cup to the person. Juan Bohorquez, whose youth had been a series of hardships and whose later life had instilled in him an ability to make humor out of bad situations, told the people with the little cannon this was what was required to bring everyone together – a communal celebration in the name of the Holy Mother when the gun was fired.

Alfredo Lopez returned Lázaro's mule. He had a Winchester with him as well as a gun supported by an old scarred holster with a shell belt to match. Although Lopez was known to the villagers, because he was both taciturn and had always been disinclined to remain in San Ildefonso any longer than he had to, no one had ever developed more than a passing acquaintanceship with him. His arrival now was soberly considered by people because he had not returned alone. The boy who accompanied him was no more than possibly ten or twelve years old. No one knew him, and Alfredo Lopez made no introductions, except to say the child was a very good shot with the Winchester, and that his name was Guillermo.

Patrick Flaherty, the stranded freighter, asked Lopez why he had brought the child, and Lopez, four inches taller than the freighter, looked gravely down as he replied: 'I caught him finally. He has been living like an animal. I've seen him a few times. When I caught him a few days ago, he told me he was left behind when his parents were crossing toward Alta California and they had six other children. His father is a *gringo*. He named the boy William.'

Flaherty gazed at the lad, who stood as close to Alfredo Lopez as he could, clearly anxious and frightened. Flaherty fished in a pocket, brought forth a twist of licorice root, and held it out. The boy took it and mumbled something as he began chewing.

Torres Mendoza stopped, stared, then raised a quizzical glance. 'He is yours?' he asked of the gaunt, tall man.

Lopez hesitated briefly before nodding. He took the boy by the arm and led him away.

Mendoza watched them. 'I didn't know Lopez had a family.'

The Irishman had something else in mind. 'What's the latest news? An old woman at the upper end of town told me we are surrounded by raiders.'

Torres Mendoza snorted. 'She is *loco en la cabeza*. Do you have weapons?'

'Just my pistol. My rifle was in the wagon. Is it true the soldiers let the Mexicans go south with my wagon?'

'It is true. Where have you been?'

Flaherty ignored the question. 'If I don't get my animals an' wagon back, someone's goin' to have to pay for 'em.'

Mendoza's teeth shone in the darkness when he smiled. '*Señor,* you should worry about yourself.' After he had told the freighter this, he walked away.

Father Damion returned from scouting. He informed Lázaro that he had seen nothing, but with the brilliant glare of the warning fire in his face it did not mean that they were not out there.

Lázaro worried about the saloonman who had also gone out scouting. When he encountered Rafael Cardinal, carrying a rifle and with a pair of bandoleers crossed over his chest the way marauders wore them, he was about to remonstrate about the bandoleers on the grounds that they had for many years been the symbol of border jumpers

93

and wearing them now could very well get Rafael Cardinál shot in error. He did not get the chance to speak. Cardinál said: 'There are horses west of here. It could be riders, or maybe they are loose. I was out there beyond the alley and heard them. If it is riders, they are coming toward us. We should put men over there with guns.'

Lázaro told Cardinál to find someone to go with them. Cardinál left, and Lázaro walked southward, the direction raiders used coming up out of Mexico. There were some women with rifles down here. Two old men greeted Lázaro, saying it was their job to watch southward, which they had been doing when the women arrived. Clearly, the old men strongly disapproved.

One of the women was Isabel Montenegro. She did not hear what the old men said, but her defiant stance indicated that she suspected. Lázaro told her the women should get behind buildings, a harmless suggestion. The woman replied fiercely. 'This is better. If they come, we can face them.'

Lázaro dryly replied: 'And get yourselves killed.'

Before Isabel Montenegro could respond, one of the other women made a squeaky sound, and several rifles were swung westward where a man called softly: 'Be at ease. I am Juan Bohorquez.'

The women did not lower their rifles, but

one of them spoke tartly. 'And I am *Señora* Lopez de Santa Anna. Show yourself!'

The saloonman came out of the night, sounding disgusted. 'What are you doing? If you had the sense *el Dios* gave a goose, you would lie flat on the ground. You are targets, standing like you are.'

Lázaro spoke before he could make out little more than details. There was only one other person in San Ildefonso who was nearly as broad as he was tall and rolled slightly when he walked. 'What did you find?'

'I saw the priest and then lost him,' Bohorquez replied irritably. 'What is this ... women making targets of themselves?' Bohorquez halted in front of Lázaro. 'The raiders' horses are hobbled, or I could have stampeded them. They have guards with the remuda. Both are either drunk or asleep. I could have cut their throats. Has the holy man returned?'

Lázaro nodded. 'Yes. How many are out there?'

'By the horses I would say about twenty. I could hear them. Otherwise being alone it would be suicide to crawl any farther. Lázaro, there must be more. Maybe camped somewhere else. You and I could scout northward and curve around southerly on the east side. If there are no more than the ones I saw, we could make up a force from the village and attack them.'

Isabel Montenegro interrupted to say: 'My son's wife has a mother.'

Bohorquez, looking startled, said: 'It is the law of God that everyone has a mother.'

Isabel ignored the saloonman to address Lázaro Guardia. 'The *indio* is with my son ... her daughter.'

Lázaro waited in silence as did Juan Bohorquez. It was harder for the saloonman. Isabel, to him, was making no sense.

'She knows every rock for a hundred miles. She is a thin, wiry person. Take her scouting with you. It is said they can see better at night than we can.'

Lázaro nodded, took Juan by the arm, and went back northward. Where he released his grip, they were in front of the Forthright Stage & Freight Company's corral yard. Juan looked darkly at his companion.

Lázaro spoke before Bohorquez could. 'North up the roadway. If we find nothing, then we go out a way and around southeastward. One thing worries me.'

'The damned Indian woman?'

'Never mind the Indian. Worry about getting shot by our friends!'

Bohorquez evidently did not consider this much of a risk, because he jerked his head and began walking.

The moon was slanting away. In the northwest the night would be cooling. On the south desert summer nights cooled only slightly, and beyond that point did not get cooler. Moonlight was only a disadvantage to people who worked best in pitch darkness. This particular night the moon was shaped like a curved sword and was only slightly thicker than most half moons are. There was almost no noise. San Ildefonso had all day and most of the night to imagine graphically what was coming, and it was nothing people were inclined to discuss, even among close friends.

Patrick Flaherty had deserted from the Army nine years earlier. In seeking a place where he had little chance of being found and arrested, he had chosen New Mexico Territory, because he had heard it was a place where people who wished to be ignored would be. What he had found was an uneasy existence. New Mexico was a territory, not a state, and territories were administered by the Army. Nine years was a long time. He had been freighting for six of those nine years, had encountered soldier patrols often – and was, indeed, ignored.

His present predicament aroused the old uneasiness. There was a stockaded fort not too many miles southeast of San Ildefonso, and, if there was one thing he had learned as a soldier, it was that this kind of situation, which now existed south of the border and north of it as well, brought soldiers out in great numbers, comparable to what happened when a beehive was struck with a stick.

If he could have left, he would have. However, not only had he been set afoot, but his years of saving money to buy the wagon and the mules represented the loss of his capital outlay and his way of making a living. When he was handed a rifle and ammunition by a woman with a rock-set to her jaw and a challenging glare from her eyes, he had accepted the armament, and even thanked her.

Flaherty was sitting on a bench out front of the *curandero's* small and unkempt *jacal* when two men came abreast, each armed to the teeth. He knew them both. He knew the saloonman best.

He called in English because he had almost no command of Spanish, nine years of being in a predominantly Spanish-speaking territory notwithstanding.

Juan Bohorquez answered the greeting. 'Come with us, *yanqui*. We are going to see who might be out there.'

Flaherty made no move to leave the bench. 'If you see my mules, let me know an' I'll steal 'em back.'

He watched the two men continue northward, when out of nowhere an undersized boy came soundlessly to share the bench and ask if Flaherty had another licorice stick. Flaherty had two more sticks. He gave the boy one stick and began chewing the other stick himself. He looked around. The boy's feet did not reach the ground. He said: 'How old are you?'

'Eleven, maybe twelve, I think. You have a name, *señor?*'

'Mister Flaherty. How about you? You have a name?'

The lad chewed half a minute before replying. 'William Colson. The goat man calls me Guillermo. Do you know why?'

'No.'

'Guillermo is Spanish for William. Do you understand Spanish?'

'No. Why should I? This territory belongs to the United States. Americans speak English. You speak it.'

'My father spoke it.' The youth removed the licorice root and considered Flaherty. 'He might come back for me.'

'How long ago did he leave you?'

'Many months. I don't know except that it was winter.'

'Did your ma know?'

'She was very sick and coughed all the time.'

'Did she know, boy?'

'I ... don't want to think so. She was very sick.'

Alfredo Lopez appeared, jerked his head at the boy, ignored Flaherty, and walked south with the boy at his side.

Chapter Seven

When Men Are Desperate

It may have been an inherent ability, then again it may have been an acquired one. Men such as Juan Bohorquez with physical strength and confidence, born of a few failures and many successes, provided they reached maturity, had been – and many still were – *guerrilleros*. The saloonman was as agile as a cat. Lázaro was impressed how Bohorquez utilized every shadow, every dark place to achieve concealment for them both. He went north soundlessly and warily. When it appeared to Lázaro Guardia that, if there had been marauders out here, they would have found them, Juan Bohorquez altered course slightly in an easterly direction for a short distance, then southward.

At times they heard voices from the village. Some idiot was singing about cockroaches. Someone, who was not an idiot, very abruptly shut him up.

Juan Bohorquez was more interested in horses than in men. He paused often to listen. It was at one of these places, perhaps several hundred feet easterly from the village, that Juan paused to listen, started to move again, and suddenly stopped. Lázaro could see watery moonlight reflecting off a gun barrel. Seconds passed. Bohorquez moved a foot at a time, like a stalking cat. Lázaro had the prudence to remain where they had stopped, without moving.

A voice hissed in swift Spanish. For seconds that was the only sound before a second voice replied, also in Spanish but not in a whisper.

Lázaro heard that man. He had said something about there being no privacy when one had to pass water. His voice was slightly hoarse, and he blurred his words.

The one who hissed like a snake gave an order. Evidently it wasn't obeyed as he thought it should've been, because there was the sound of a blow and someone's groan.

Lázaro inched ahead. Juan Bohorquez had a short man by the jacket in back and was punching him along. The short man seemed in too much pain to stand upright. When they reached Lázaro, he asked Juan if he had hit the *bandolero* and got back a curt reply. 'With my knee in the *cajones*. He doesn't need them anyway. Look at him. He is old.'

Juan shoved the prisoner in the direction of the village. The prisoner had a pair of shell belts crossed over his chest. He occasionally groaned and shortened his steps, but he did not attempt to stop or to speak.

Lázaro hiked ahead to call out and identify

himself. The response was a very deep silence. He continued to identify himself until he could make out the brass cannon and several motionless people standing with it.

Torres Mendoza a little more than raised his voice when he called back, addressing Juan Bohorquez. 'Where did you get that piece of *carroña?*'

The saloonman answered gruffly. 'Getting rid of too much *pulque.*' He lifted away the captive's holstered Colt. 'Gag him, so that his friends can't hear the bastard, and hang him.'

Alfredo Lopez stepped toward the captive, who was easily six inches shorter, and said: 'Push his head in a trough. I've seen him before, but without the crossed shell belts.'

The prisoner squinted at the tall man. 'I don't know you,' he mumbled.

Lopez replied curtly. 'Yes, you do. You rider of other people's horses. I saw you steal my horse and ride away on him. Three years ago. I couldn't chase you on foot, and I didn't have my gun.'

The old marauder squinted hard at Alfredo Lopez. 'Did you know that horse would bite?'

'I knew. He waited until you had a foot in the stirrup then swung his head. I close-reined him on the off side so he couldn't turn his head.'

The older man said: 'He bit me so bad on my behind I couldn't ride for two months.'

Juan considered the *guerrillero*. 'How many

like you are out there?'

'Five. To scout. Our camp is south some miles.'

'They will come in the morning?'

The man nodded. 'Before sunrise.'

Torres Mendoza asked the prisoner's name. Before he could reply, the saloonman growled: 'Take him away and hang him.'

It was done. Alfredo Lopez supplied the rope from someone's outbuilding.

Juan took three men and scouted again. He was gone almost until the moon departed, found no more marauders, and returned, leading a stray horse he had found. Buckled on the right side of the *silla* was a gun boot containing a long-barreled shotgun. The animal was off-saddled, unbridled, and turned loose.

The villagers became groups with rifles, willing artillerymen with the little cannon, scouts and sentinels, and, having been so many hours preparing, they individually knew to which group they belonged. Only the freighter had any knowledge of organized fighting, and he offered no advice.

Before the prisoner had been hanged, he had told them from where he had stood under a barn balkhead that his band of raiders numbered thirty. He had also told them something they already knew – that Mexican soldiers were in pursuit of revolutionaries over the border into New Mexico

103

Territory, and other bands of *guerrilleros* were also up over the border.

Maria Alvarez appeared, wild-eyed, gray hair in her face, carrying her dead husband's Sharps rifle for which she had no bullets and so went around asking for some. No one provided her with charges for two reasons. One, bullets for that old rifle were not readily available, and, second, if there was fighting, of which no one had a doubt, there was the possibility that the agitated old *loca* would shoot the wrong people.

It was long past midnight when those able to rest were brought to their feet by a bugle. Whatever call it sounded, there was no doubt that the bugler was experienced in the use of his instrument. Among San Ildefonso's inhabitants no one had ever before heard of *guerrilleros* using a bugle.

Alfredo Lopez thought those *Federales* he had seen and heard the night before were returning. Lázaro and Father Damion discussed the possibility of the village being caught between soldiers and marauders, in which case there would be monumental confusion.

Lázaro had been going among the defenders, warning of the consequences if they allowed the attackers to get into the village to hide among the *jacales*. The most adamant against infiltration were the women at the lower end of San Ildefonso who had chosen Isabel Montenegro as their leader.

The bugler, whoever and wherever he was, did not make another call. A gradual conviction spread that the bugler had to have been a soldier, which meant there were Mexican regulars close by.

After the bugle sounded, there were few people who slept. Maria Alvarez in a frenzy of delight told anyone who would listen that a Mexican route army was invading New Mexico to take back from the United States all the land it had lost after the Mexican War.

By this time, and as Maria's stories became less believable, her ability for adding to the fear and dread diminished. But no one doubted an attack would come. An old border jumper, hanging limply from a balkhead near the upper end of town, gave grim truth to the fact that marauders were facing San Ildefonso from the south. It did not help, either, that the sound of horses in a westerly direction implied either part of the southern band or perhaps an independent band of raiders was waiting for enough visibility to storm the village from that direction.

Efraim Montoya, momentarily down from his perch on the *cantina* roof, suggested that an attack be launched against the southerly invaders before sunrise. Father Damion had a blunt comment about that. 'And if the raiders west of us attack while we are fighting below town, what then?'

Pat Flaherty spat amber and shook his head. He told Torres Mendoza it was like watching a bunch of chickens with a fox in their yard. Everyone had suggestions, and no one had any idea how skirmishes were fought.

Mendoza, who had little affection for *gringos,* asked: 'You could do better?'

Patrick Flaherty looked long and hard at Mendoza before walking away without saying another word.

Stone sober, José Montenegro, standing in shadows near the little cannon, cursed the *gringo* soldiers. He found others who felt the same way without knowing the soldiers were responsible for their present predicament. They cursed them because, not counting small groups of patrols, the *norteamericano* Army rarely appeared when it was needed. And of a certainty it was very much needed now.

Lázaro met the saloonman when he returned again from scouting, this time with no captive. Bohorquez said loudly, if the attack came from the west, the cannon would be useless. Not only was it very heavy, but where it should have wheels, it had a wooden sled with steel runners. Lázaro considered Bohorquez's powerful physique and thought that if the saloonman could find enough defenders of equal strength and keep them in the alley, when fighting started, they should be able to maneuver the gun. Bohorquez flapped his arms, but Lázaro told him now to assemble some strong men and stay with the cannon.

Rafael Cardinál searched for Lázaro to say he had scouted southward where there was the dying fire of a bivouac and had seen something that chilled his blood. 'They have a crank gun mounted on wheels.'

'A what?'

'One of those crank guns with many barrels. The *gringos* use them. They must have stolen this one from the *gringos*. A man stands behind it and turns a crank so that all the barrels revolve while they are firing.' Rafael Cardinál flung his arms wide. 'With that thing they can kill a hundred people.'

Lázaro remembered seeing such a gun. The *norteamericanos* called it a Gatling gun. As Cardinál was turning away, Lázaro caught his sleeve, told him to find Juan Bohorquez, and bring him to Lázaro. This was accomplished, and, as Lázaro faced Bohorquez he asked if Rafael Cardinál had told him about the crank gun. He had. The saloonman wiped sweat off his face, and it was not that warm a night.

Lázaro asked Rafael Cardinál if he could find the crank gun in darkness, and, when he got an affirmative reply, Lázaro faced Juan Bohorquez. 'We have to find that gun and destroy it, which means we have to sneak up on the *guerrilleros* in their blankets.'

107

Bohorquez said: 'Now?'

'Now!'

'But you told me to stay with the cannon.'

'Get your strong men, come to the lower end of the village. Find Torres. Have him bring another ten men or so.'

Mendoza arrived with his forces, mindful of the attackers west of the village, and would have protested, but Lázaro gave him no chance. 'Now!' he told them. 'The darkness will not be here much longer. *Go!*'

Lázaro led them to the southerly end of San Ildefonso and was challenged by one of Isabel Montenegro's *amazonas*. Isabel appeared, wearing a machete on her left side and a holstered colt on her right side. She also had one of the long-barreled rifles. Lázaro explained about the crank gun and his intention of taking these men either to steal it or to destroy it.

Bohorquez and Mendoza explained about the Gatling gun. One of the men the saloonman had brought was Isabel Montenegro's son, Leonides, whose Indian wife had recently foaled. Isabel's face was expressionless as Lázaro led the way through the jumble of crates, furniture, and other pieces of bulwark the women had erected. He did not look back and neither did Isabel's son, but she stood like a stone, watching them, Leonides in particular. She and her man had had only one child.

The moon was nearly gone. It had cast little light anyway. Lázaro speculated that false dawn would arrive within an hour or so, to be followed by sunrise. Whether he and his followers succeeded or failed, they needed darkness to escape back the way they had come. After dawn light they would be easy targets.

Rafael Cardinál moved without haste and especially without noise. Those following did the same. When they eventually detected the smoke scent of a dying fire, Lázaro brushed Rafael's arm and asked about sentries. Cardinál shook his head. 'I think there are none. Why should there be? Only crazy people would leave their village to attack *guerrilleros*.' Cardinál smiled as he resumed the stalk.

The smoke scent grew stronger. Lázaro thought they had walked almost two miles, and the passage of time worried him. Once the faint, fish-belly paleness of false dawn appeared, they would be exposed. He was beginning to think what they were doing was foolhardy, when Rafael abruptly dropped flat. Lázaro and their companions did the same. A man appeared, walking unsteadily. He passed within twenty feet of them. He was hatless and his clothes rumpled. He had no shell belt or side-arm.

They waited until the man walked back, less unsteady this time as he passed, and Lázaro's heart stopped for seconds when the man looked easterly where they were lying. That fright passed as the man went around the Gatling gun to his blankets and lowered himself until they could no longer see him.

As they rose, Rafael pointed. The crank gun was pointing northward. Its wheels had been chocked, although why that should be no one could say. This was flat country. The gun could not run away if it wanted to.

Juan Bohorquez had told no one what he carried inside his shirt until they stood, looking at lumpy outlines of border jumpers. Juan sneered and whispered. 'Too much *pulque* and too little brains.' He fished inside his shirt as he went to the gun. The others could not clearly see what he was doing until he lighted the fuse and yelled: 'Run!'

They ran. Lázaro saw Juan Bohorquez catching up and called to him: 'Why didn't you tell us?'

'Because the chance was good it might blow us up, too.' Juan was not built for speed, and, although his chest was wide and deep, Lázaro could hear him sucking air even as Juan began to fall back. They ran like hares, but even so it was possible to look back and see the sputtering fuse, something that made them run faster.

When the explosion occurred, reverberations shook the ground, and even at a respectable distance the shock seemed like someone pushing against their backs. The explosion was loud enough, but in the night its echoes seemed to chase one another for a long time.

Lázaro called for a halt. The last man to come up was Juan Bohorquez, and he sank to the ground, breathing loudly. When Torres Mendoza came to him and asked if he was all right, Juan Bohorquez looked up and replied through rattling gasps: 'Why didn't Morisco tell me?'

'Tell you what?'

'That one stick would be enough.'

'How many did you have?'

'Two.'

In the south they could hear men yelling. Lázaro used a moment of rest to wonder how close that man's bedroll was to the crank gun – the man who had walked unsteadily away from the camp to micturate. Such an explosion could be heard for a great distance. Perhaps as far as Chinle. The sound of horsemen followed the wake of the explosion. Lázaro stood, listening. The riders were coming straight toward them. He led the way eastward, and again Juan Bohorquez was barely able to keep up. As he ran and gasped, he interspersed his gasps with profanity in two languages.

The riders passed about a quarter of a mile in a westerly direction. Lázaro thought of unprepared San Ildefonso and led off in a steady trot. Whatever happened at the village would certainly occur before they got back, which made it seem to Lázaro that destroying the crank gun might not have been a good idea, after all.

They had to stop several times, and at each stop they listened to the night in breathless silence. It was Bohorquez, pumping air like a bellows, who yelled for them to hasten. As they did so, Bohorquez eventually began to lose ground and swear loudly at the same time.

They had covered more than two-thirds of the distance when there was a rattle of gunfire up ahead. Torres Mendoza yelled something about the women and their barricade. Lázaro altered course again, this time moving westerly. If the marauders turned back, he wanted to be behind them.

Gunfire up ahead made flash points of muzzle blast that were visible to the exhausted runners. Later, they could discern dark outlines of buildings. False dawn was increasing visibility by the minute.

San Ildefonso looked and sounded like a battlefield. Muzzle blasts shown for fractions of a second from so many different places Lázaro began to hope the raiders would be chased away. Juan Bohorquez used his bull-bass voice to yell that he and his companions were approaching, something that may have confused the defenders, most of whom had no idea that Lázaro had led his companions on the southward raid.

Juan continued to yell, and eventually the others did the same. Much of the gunfire at the lower end of the village stopped, except for an occasional shot. When Lázaro and the others reached the barricade and began scrambling over it, Isabel Montenegro watched them pass until a particular one sprawled in the dust, when part of the barricade he had been climbing over collapsed. She ran to the fallen man, calling his name. When he rose, leaning to pick up his Winchester, Isabel cried out in anguish. The man straightened up, avoided his mother's arms, and spoke only a few words before loping after his companions. He said: 'If it had been a girl, I would have named it for you.'

San Ildefonso under attack was a place of movement and turmoil, yelling and gunfire. The day was being grudgingly born, and, when visibility was good enough, the defenders used every scrap of shelter they could find to fire from. The enraged *guerrilleros*, firing from horseback, were not only excellent targets, they had another distinct advantage. Shooting from the hurricane deck of a running horse was almost a guarantee that there would be few casualties.

While the fight lasted, the noise was deafening. Men yelled, fired their weapons, called back and forth, and turned the air blue with profanity. It ended almost as quickly as it had

113

begun. Excepting a few desultory gunshots spread over long interludes of quiet, it was finished.

José Montenegro walked to the center of the roadway and strode southward. His six-gun dangled from one hand. His stride was unsteady, and someone called from the semi-gloom for him to get out of the roadway. He seemed not to hear. Crazy Maria Alvarez flew into the road, rags flapping, struck Isabel's husband at the knees. When he fell backwards atop the old woman, someone fired a gun. The bullet struck the front of Moses Morisco's store near where José would have been, if he had been standing. He cursed and jerked as Maria Alvarez called endearing entreaties while extricating herself. Several men went to help José upright. Maria threw her arms around him, calling him Feliciano, which was not the name of her husband who had vanished.

Several villagers grappled with the old woman, dragging her away while those with José Montenegro watched. The wrinkled old *curandero* peered intently at José Montenegro and observed: *'Pulque,* you idiot.'

José looked down his nose at the *curandero*. 'Tequila, you antiquated horse's ass.'

They led José back where he was supposed to be. Francesca Cardinál sighed. 'Sober! He has not been sober in fifteen years!'

114

Chapter Eight

The Surround

When there was no more gunfire, people began warily to appear. Efraim Montoya went to his house and returned to the roadway, carrying his medicine bundle. It may have been – as some said – a miracle that no one was killed, but there were several wounded. Those unable to walk were carried to the *cantina*. Father Damion was there with beads dangling from the same hand he used to make the sign of the four corners of the Cross and offered prayers. He was without his stole. There had been no time to go to the mission for it.

The freighter proved to be an uncommon nurse. He insisted on using basins of hot water and an armload of clean rags. Efraim Montoya's nose was out of joint. Several times the freighter growled for him to get out of the way.

Montoya did manage to care for a man with a chest injury. He sent for a chicken, and, when it was brought, he wrung its neck, then split it open, and placed it complete with warm entrails over the wound. It would, he assured the wounded defender, draw out the poison and bad blood and prevent infection.

Isabel Montenegro and her *amazonas* went among the buildings, seeking casualties. They brought in white-headed Tomás Henriques. He had been grazed across the shoulder which would normally not have prevented him from walking, but he had lost blood and something, shock probably, kept him from walking. Isabel had heard him praying before the effigy above the altar at the church. She and another robust woman had half dragged, half carried him to the *cantina*.

There were six others wounded, but only one, a man shot in the lung, was seriously injured. He was out of his head some of the time. It was Alfred Lopez, the goat man who had killed the *Federale*. Sitting on the floor close to this injured man was the undersized Guillermo, to whom no one paid much attention. He rocked back and forth very slightly. His ragged clothing had blood showing, but he would not allow himself to be examined, and no one insisted. There was enough work for all those doing the caring to spend much time with a ragged boy, sitting on the floor.

Lázaro, Juan Bohorquez, and Torres Mendoza went warily among the buildings on the west side. There were four riderless horses, wandering out there. They found three dead raiders and one with a broken leg who tried unsuccessfully to hide in a dilapidated sty. They dragged him outside, where he begged for his life, and shot him.

The fight was over. Daylight was brightening the world. The defenders could see a dust banner southward. Evidently the marauders were heading for their distant camp.

Juan Bohorquez thought they would gather the rest of their crew and return. Lázaro doubted it – not in broad daylight – and he was right. The attackers did not return.

Tomás Henriques was cared for and bandaged. He moved out of the *cantina* and sat alone in a corner of Morisco's store with a bottle from which he occasionally sipped. When Moses Morisco came in, the white-headed man remarked: 'They say you ordered all those guns from a trader in Santa Fé. Tell me. Why would you order so many guns?'

Morisco hadn't ordered the guns and said so. Henriques sipped, gazed at Morisco, and made a good guess. 'Someone, then, ordered them to be delivered to you, in your name.'

Moses Morisco could add nothing to that theory, but he inclined his head. Such things happened. As he was turning away, the white-headed man spoke again. 'Do you think we may win?'

Morisco looked down. 'We have to win, but it is in the hands of God.'

Henriques raised hard, black eyes. 'Do you believe in God?'

Morisco frowned. 'Everyone believes in God. What kind of a question is that?'

'*Guerrilleros* don't.'

'You know that? What do they pray to?'

'*Señor* Winchester and *Señor* Colt.'

Moses Morisco walked away.

Father Damion came to Henriques and eyed him briefly before speaking. 'Does the wound hurt?'

'Yes.'

'If it had been lower and more to the center ... Tomás, how many times have I asked you to confess?'

Henriques gazed steadily at the priest. 'I told you, Father, with my last breath.' He got to his feet and walked away.

Father Damion sighed.

Guillermo came to tug at the priest's sleeve and jerked his head. Father Damion allowed himself to be led back to a gloomy corner of the *cantina* where the goat man from west of the village was motionless on some bloody blankets. A disemboweled chicken was lying nearby, and someone had tried clumsily to stop the leaking blood with rags. Father Damion knelt, spoke, got no answer, peeked at the wound, and settled back on his heels. When he looked, Guillermo was white-faced. Beside, and slightly behind the boy, Pat Flaherty stood without expression as Father

118

Damion rose. The priest looked over the lad's head toward the freighter and spoke three words about Alfredo Lopez: 'He is dead.'

The boy's knees buckled. He placed a grimy small hand on the face of Alfredo Lopez and without success tried to choke back the tears. When Father Damion would have led the boy away by the shoulder, he would not budge and, when the priest would have used more force, Flaherty said: 'Leave him be, Father.'

Alfredo Lopez proved to be the only fatality. As knowledge of his death circulated, those caring for the injured became both solemn and silent.

Lázaro and Juan Bohorquez conferred briefly. Between them it was agreed that the wounded were more secure in the saloon where the mud walls were three feet thick. As this was being discussed, one of the lads who had been sent to scout came to Juan Bohorquez and told him that from the roof top of the general store he had seen a distant dust banner, approaching from the northwest.

Lázaro sent the lad back to watch and told Torres Mendoza what the lad had seen. Torres Mendoza was skeptical. 'In broad daylight?'

Lázaro shrugged. 'What matters is that they are coming?'

'Who, then, *compadre?*'

'Maybe the *Federales.* That's the direction in

which they rode yesterday. Toward Chinle.'

Torres Mendoza made a bitter smile. 'Good. They will come onto the murdering bastards to the west and those down south.'

Lázaro asked a question. 'How many?'

'How would I know?'

'If I am right, between the bands of raiders there will be more men than there are *Federales*.'

Torres Mendoza nodded. 'Maybe. Fine. They will fight each other.'

'And what happens to whoever wins?'

'San Ildefonso...?'

'Get Morisco's spy glass and keep watch to the north. Whatever you see, come and tell me.'

'We could push the cannon to the north end, Lázaro.'

'*Sí*, we could. Torres, what is our worst danger?'

'The *guerrilleros*. What kind of a thing is that to ask someone?'

'If the *Federales* were chasing them...?'

'It is against the law for them to be in New Mexico.'

As though there had been no interruption, Lázaro Guardia continued speaking and shocked Torres Mendoza into total silence by saying: 'When the *Federales* get close, coming from the north, they will meet the *guerrilleros* west of here. When that happens, we should be ready to join them.'

'Join the *Federales?*'

'We aren't strong enough to win against both bands of invaders. Get the spy glass and watch.'

Torres Mendoza departed, moving like a sleepwalker.

From the east there was a gunshot. It encouraged every villager who was aboard to seek shelter, fast. Rafael Cardinál took a mirror from the store, went behind the loading dock, and flashed reflected sunlight in the direction from which the gunshot had come. If Cardinál's idea was to attract a gunshot, it succeeded, but there were two gunshots. The source of one of the gunshots was a bushwhacking Mexican who sprang up straight into the air and collapsed against the bush from which he had tried to do some sniping. This baffled everyone for some time since the shot that had killed the marauder had seemed to come from the north, from the extreme upper end of the village. Of course, there were armed villagers up there, but something about the killing shot hadn't sounded as though it had come from among those buildings.

The shrivelled *curandero*, again atop the saloon, appeared near the front of the building, gesturing with both arms and calling in Spanish.

There was further bewilderment until Father Damion squinted in the direction of the mission and spoke aside to Rafael Cardinál. 'The bell tower. Watch, he will move.'

Rafael watched, but there was no movement. He left to join the men on the east side who were straining hard to find another ambusher out there.

Evidently the man who had been killed had been alone. There were no more gunshots, but there was increasing heat, as the day wore along to the time when men stood in their shadows.

Several women worked together making a meal. The aroma inclined some of the defenders to leave their posts to get fed. Nothing was said about this until Isabel Montenegro arrived and, with her machete and pistol, glowered at the diners. They ignored her, so she went to one of the cooking pots and dumped it on the ground. That got their attention. When the swearing diminished, and those who had no longer had pleats in their stomachs, stamped angrily away, the remaining people threatened Isabel Montenegro with knives. She left them to find her husband.

José was sitting on a small keg, hands locked, head down. When his wife appeared, he looked up long enough to say: 'What am I supposed to do? It is hot, the cannon is pointing in the wrong direction, and everyone has left me to guard it.' José made a sweeping gesture with one arm. 'Guard this thing that no one can move!'

'Where did you get the bottle?'

'I don't have a bottle.'

'You've been drinking, José.'

'I went to pray ... we may all be killed. I went to the mission to ask for God's mercy.'

'You took church wine?'

José slumped, re-clasped his hands, and would not speak. His wife left the alley.

The *gringo* freighter was in shade with Guillermo. Isabel watched as the man taught the lad, whom he called by his English name, William, how to shoulder and aim a rifle. She heard the abrupt sound when the boy pulled the trigger to dry-fire the gun.

She went in search of her son, who was at his *jacal* with his wife and their child. There was another woman there, the mother of the Indian Isabel's son had married. She was tall, angular, and expressionless. She did not speak, nor would she, until Isabel spoke first.

Something occurred that had previously happened with the identical result: someone blew a bugle. For ten seconds no one moved, then there was a rush to the west side of the village. Word passed swiftly that the Mexican soldiers were returning, but strain as they did, no one saw *Federales* or even a dust banner.

Lázaro told Juan Bohorquez if there was anyone in San Ildefonso who could blow a bugle, or for that matter owned one, he had never heard of it, and he had been born and raised in the village.

Juan lost interest quickly. One of the lads atop Morisco's store was waving his arms. Northward on top of the cantina Efraim Montoya was doing the same. Torres Mendoza came from the upper end of the village with Moses Morisco's collapsible spy glass to say *someone* was approaching, but even with the spy glass all he could make out were horsemen and dust.

'How far away?' Lázaro asked, and Torres Mendoza gestured. He had no idea how far it was. Lázaro sent Mendoza and Bohorquez to get every horse they could find, and riders for each horse. Torres Mendoza screwed up his face. 'Join them, Lázaro? They will fire on us. They have no friends up here, only enemies.'

Montoya, atop the saloon, was now waving both arms and jumping up and down. '¡Soldados! ¡Soldados! An army of them ... go and see for yourselves.'

People were scattering like quail, mostly toward the west side of the village, all with guns. Lázaro scowled. If it were Mexican soldiers, and if the *bandoleros* were still out there somewhere, they would surely fire on the soldiers. Well, what did it matter? As Torres Mendoza had said, no one had friends here, only enemies.

The bugle sounded again, and this time, because Lázaro was facing northerly, he thought he knew about where the bugler was, but before he could do more than speculate, there was an irregular scatter of gunfire. Lázaro crossed quickly to the west side where gunsmoke was lazily rising in the still air.

Francesca Cardinál, sweaty and furiously trying to dislodge a swollen brass casing before plugging in another one, saw Lázaro and said: 'We will hurt them, *jefe*.'

Lázaro wagged his head. 'Not at that distance. Let them get closer.' But this did not happen. The Mexican soldiers were neither heroes nor fools. That long rattling fusillade from among the buildings and its accompanying long cloud of smoke would have convinced an idiot that San Ildefonso was well defended. The soldiers veered farther west, behind their saber-waving officer. They had been out of range before, and shortly after they reined farther, so they could not be reached even by rifles.

What some of the defenders had been musing about happened. As the *Federales* loped past with the village on their left at a considerable distance, a deafening roll of gunfire erupted farther west, smoke rose, and *bandoleros* appeared in agitated excitement, continuing to fire. This time the soldiers were within range. As *Federales* were shot out of their saddles, Pat Flaherty spoke from Lázaro's left side. 'Damned fools, they put out no scouts, no outriders.'

125

Lázaro did not acknowledge hearing that statement. He watched the soldiers break and scatter, riding for their lives. He almost felt sorry for them.

The ambushing renegades continued to fire even after their targets were beyond range. The soldiers, with no longer a sword-waving officer to lead them, lost all semblance of order. It was clearly every man for himself. As Lázaro and the freighter watched, a large sorrel horse went end over end like a pinwheel, hurling his rider into the air where he landed on his back, still clutching a rifle. The horse scrambled to its feet and ran, stirrups flopping, reins in the air.

The watchers waited for the soldier to rise. He never did, for the best of all reasons. His neck was broken.

Villagers, mostly women, continued to fire even though the border jumpers they fired at were far too distant to be hit. The freighter went among them, shouting for them to stop firing. They did, but not immediately – they were too agitated, too upset and angry.

When the last of the *Federales* were well south of the village, clearly with Old Mexico as their destination, Lázaro went back to the roadway and between two adobes where men were grunting and swearing. A villager saw him and yelled. 'Out there. To the west. Using the brush for cover. Watch.'

Lázaro watched as the cannoneers con-

126

tinued to strain at turning their cannon. He saw two riders, sitting in the distance, reins slack.

He told the gunners not to waste a charge. Several excited villagers glared and shouted back. He could not understand, so he went forward, roughly shoved several men aside, and came face to face with a sweaty José Montenegro who was interested in nothing but having his gun aimed as he wanted it to be.

Lázaro grabbed him by the shoulder, spun him around, and José, sobering up and agitated, gave Lázaro a hard push. Two men caught him, kept him from falling. José returned to aiming. When he was satisfied, he straightened up, called for the sputtering linstock, and commanded: '¡Fuero!'

The earth shook. The little gun sprang backwards six feet. Deafened defenders were stunned. Out where those riders had been, and for several *varas* on both sides, tough underbrush flew into the air amid an impenetrable cloud of dun dust through which villagers on the east side of San Ildefonso could make out fleeing men, some howling, but mostly simply running as though *Señor Satán* was at their heels.

José Montenegro looked balefully at Lázaro and spat. As with the others in the vicinity of the cannon, José had seen men sneaking through brush. A considerable number of them. Lázaro had seen only two mounted men. He had incorrectly assumed they were scouts.

People came from the west side to the east side. The little cannon's explosion had rattled the ground even beyond the west side of the village, and those ambushing renegades far to the west had probably also felt the reverberations. Surely they had heard the cannon when it was fired. Wise men would have been daunted.

Moses Morisco appeared, wearing some kind of apron tucked inside his britches. When the priest arrived, the storeman said: 'God is with us.'

Father Damion put a skeptical glance on Morisco when he replied: 'Tell me that tomorrow, old friend.'

Morisco made a wan smile and waddled away.

Afternoon arrived, as it commonly did, with a burnished sky of heat-faded yellow, and a sun that wilted everything it touched. The need now was not for food or rest. It was for water.

José Montenegro, hard-eyed and fierce, gathered six men, two youths and four women, led them beyond the village to make a complete circle and return to the saloon where William was now sitting like stone beside the dead goat man. Juan Bohorquez brought José a *cerveza* that the tall man pushed away, then sat down. José neither spoke nor moved, but only gazed stonily at the mud wall.

José's wife appeared with a companion. Two women in a place where women had never been allowed. Men noticed and looked away. Isabel crossed to her husband's little table, sat down opposite him, put her head in her arms atop the table, and cried.

José's detached gaze drifted back. He leaned to place a soiled hand on her arm and say in Spanish: 'There will be never again reason for you to feel shame for me.'

She raised a face streaked with dust and tears and smiled. 'I was not so much ashamed as I was fearful it would eat your insides and kill you.'

A vengefully smiling *curandero* appeared, tanked up with water that naturally increased his sweating, and told the people in the *cantina* he had counted eleven dead *Federales* and guessed aloud that possibly as many as twenty-five had escaped. He also said there was a badly wounded *Federale* lying behind Maria Alvarez's house, if anyone cared enough to bring him to the *cantina*. There was some shuffling of feet, but no one moved toward the door until Efraim Montoya added: 'He is a *gachupín*.'

Lázaro and Father Damion exchanged a look and left the *cantina* behind the elfin *curandero*.

There were watchers – not many and mostly youths, but whatever else might happen to San Ildefonso, it would in all probability not happen on this day. Whether the fleeing soldiers and the *guerrilleros* would find water, rest, and whatever shade could be found was now up to Our Lady. The people of San Ildefonso required all those things. Dead soldiers would have to wait. Tomás Henriques, on the mission roof, had obviously recovered somewhat since he had shot a renegade scout with unerring accuracy. Yet, of all the villagers, now solemn and exhausted in the saloon, only the white headed man was not there.

Chapter Nine

A Time Of Quiet Dread

Several villagers held a parley. They were unanimous in their conviction that, since the attackers now knew they had a cannon and plenty of rifles, daylight attacks would be unwise. Lázaro thought the people should patrol beyond the village as well as among the *jacales*. He said the *guerrilleros* were *coyote*. It was his guess that they were seasoned attackers, knowing that San Ildefonso would not be an easy target as many south desert communities had been over the years. They would use dark night tactics, infiltrating if they could, and for this reason, bone weary though the defenders were, there would have to be patrols beyond the village as well as among the buildings.

The discussion was interrupted by the *gringo* freighter who told them that *la loca*, Maria Alvarez, was dead in her house. Except for the shock, nothing was said. Maria had been a tenacious annoyance with her exaggerations and her wild-eyed appearances. Most of the people knew her story. Little was said of it, and with the passage of

131

years, while Maria got crazier, her ability to make people uncomfortable had increased. Still, she was dead.

Someone asked Flaherty if she had been shot, and the freighter shook his head, no. He had found no blood. 'She's lyin' on her bed, dead as a rock. There's no blood, no sign of a fight.'

Efraim Montoya sounded solemn and knowledgeable when he said: 'It would be her heart. How old is she? Seventy? Eighty? She was always agitated. If God was willing, she should have maybe died in her sleep. Her son should be told.'

An old man flapped his arms. 'He has gone ... God knows where ... after wild horses.'

The palaver broke up. The men went about recruiting for the night watchers. At Bohorquez's saloon the news of the death of Maria Alvarez passed swiftly among the defenders. Some were saddened. Some were relieved. Father Damion said he would go to the house and give Maria the Last Rites. Efraim Montoya, interrupted in his purpose by the death of Maria Alvarez, chirped for the priest to follow him instead to where there was a wounded *gachupín*. Lázaro went along. He speculated about the wounded *gachupín* behind Maria Alvarez's house and her recent passing. It was said the Dark Angel came mostly at night.

The *curandero* led them around Maria's

house on the west side and stopped where watery light from above showed a man, lying on his side with his back to the adobe rear wall of the house. Efraim went closer and leaned. As he was straightening up, he said: 'I think he is dead.'

Lázaro and the holy man went closer. Father Damion asked: 'What is he doing back here?'

Neither of the priest's companions answered. Lázaro felt for an arm and raised it. The arm was limp and warm. He knelt and rolled the *gachupín* onto his back. Over his shoulder the priest spoke quietly. 'Joáquin Otero.'

Lázaro bent far over, held that position briefly, then leaned back to say: 'He is breathing.'

They got the unconscious man flat out on his back before they saw blood. The *gachupín* had been hit twice, once in the upper leg which appeared to be the source of most of the blood. The second injury was more serious, although there was very little bleeding. A bullet had struck Otero in the back to one side. There would be broken ribs, but the slug had passed through. Father Damion, who knew about such things, said it must have been a steel bullet. Both wounds, entrance and exit, were little more than puckered purplish swellings.

Lázaro got to his feet. Father Damion

passed from sight around the east side of the house. Moments later Lázaro and his waspish companion heard the priest's voice from inside the house without being able to distinguish the words – Father Damion was giving the Last Rites in Latin.

The *curandero,* to whom death was commonplace, thought they should leave the *gachupín* where he was lying. If they tried to move him, he would very likely hemorrhage. Lázaro considered the man whose brother had been the first casualty. He led the way back toward the center of town. There were several lighted candles among the buildings. Efraim left to carry his story to the saloon. Lázaro, about half convinced the *gachupín* would die, encountered Isabel Montenegro and told her where he had been and what he had seen. Isabel showed no concern. She and Francesca Cardinál with three other women had been among those who had scouted beyond the village, and what she had to say cleared Lázaro's mind.

'They are like ghosts. I think they went around us southward to join the other brigands.' Isabel was tired enough to sag, but with an iron spine maintained her upright, defiant stance. 'An old man scouted more than a mile southward. He swore to me he heard walking horses approaching where those men were camped when the cannon was shot off. They have all night. We gave them bad treatment. They will have *pulque* or tequila. They will come back to avenge our cannon and so many rifles firing when they ran past. *Jefe,* I know *bandoleros.* They will use darkness.'

Lázaro listened sympathetically and then went to the saloon. Only half as many people were there as had been earlier. The wounded were lined out on the floor atop old blankets. Women were with them to offer water, or something stronger if they required it.

Lázaro leaned against the bar where Juan Bohorquez eyed him with his head slightly to one side. He filled a tiny glass and set it before Lázaro, who nodded, raised it, and dropped the contents straight down.

Juan Bohorquez said: 'I sent a boy for the soldiers. I waited an hour and sent a second one.' Juan shrugged powerful shoulders without mentioning the obvious, which was simply that with renegades everywhere in the night two boys – ten boys – would need the best the Almighty had to offer to reach the *norteamericano* fort.

The scent of cooking reached even inside the cantina. Several people left. Bohorquez thought Lázaro should also go to the source of those tantalizing odors and replenish his spirit.

Lázaro said– 'They will cut throats tonight!' – and returned to the roadway, where an occasional wisp of movement told him that the defenders were among the houses.

Father Damion appeared. 'Montoya may be right. Maria died, I think, in her sleep.'

Lázaro nodded, willing to accept that. His mind was elsewhere. 'Why do they want San Ildefonso so much? We have nothing.'

'Guns,' the priest replied. 'Late model rifles with ammunition. Have you gone back up yonder?'

'To Otero? No. It seems best not to move him.'

'What you and I know, Lázaro ... if others knew he was responsible for those contraband rifles, they would tear him apart piece by piece.'

Tomás Henriques came up to say: 'I have one, *señores*. He crept into the chapel to steal the gold candlesticks from the altar and was sneaking away. I tripped him. When he fell, he cried out because the candlesticks pushed into his chest. I tied him. Do you want to see him?'

The priest and Lázaro Guardia followed old Henriques who made scarcely a sound as he led the way. He was wearing *n'de bekay* moccasins, something Lázaro had never noticed before. They had a thick protective rawhide button at the toe. In cactus country they were not as good a protection as cowhide boots, but cowhide boots at Morisco's store cost four dollars a pair.

When they found the trussed renegade near the chapel's exit door, he had almost chewed through the rawhide thongs. If they had been tanned leather, he would have escaped. Henriques yanked the prisoner to his feet and pushed him onto a bench. He took back the candlesticks and gazed bleakly at the thief.

Father Damion questioned the man who was sinewy, smelled rank and had black eyes that constantly moved. The only time they seemed venomously to brighten was when the priest asked him about his companions, and he lied which did not surprise his captors. He said there were sixty *bandoleros* with more coming from south of the border. He sneered when asked about the soldiers. He and his companions had caught three and killed them. The rest, he said, would be back in Mexico by morning; earlier if their horses held out.

When the holy man asked the question most villagers had been asking themselves – why San Ildefonso? – the prisoner said: 'There is Spanish gold hidden somewhere at the mission.'

Father Damion's eyes narrowed. He had heard that fable for as long as he had been at the mission. Dozens of men had searched, even among the old graves. He slightly shook his head. 'There is no treasure here.'

The captive's stare was unwavering, and

he smiled a little. 'You want it, *Padre?*'

'No. It is an old story. The Lord knows who started it. It is the same fable I've heard at other missions. If that's why your friends are here, let me tell you ... there is no Spanish gold. The most gold we have is those candlesticks.'

The unwashed prisoner, his hair awry, sat, watching the priest. 'We will find it,' he said eventually, 'and those who blew up our crank gun. When we leave here, there will be nothing but the dead.'

Lázaro asked a question. 'Who is Joáquin Otero?'

'He did not return. You killed him?'

The prisoner's increasingly bold attitude caused Tomás Henriques to move swiftly, lift the prisoner off the bench with his one good hand, and slam him violently against the wall. In hoarse Spanish he said: 'I have opened the bellies of better men than you will ever be. I have to clean the altar because you touched it. *Bastardo,* I will break you with my hands!' The old man rammed the prisoner back onto the bench, leaned his face close, and growled: 'Do you know about making you barefoot and clubbing you to walk across a bed of coals?'

The prisoner now had reason to fear for his life, and it showed. Even after the priest got between them, the prisoner leaned to keep an eye on the old man. Lázaro gently tugged Henriques away and said: 'He will die but not by you. Keep your hands clean.'

The old man loosened a bit at a time, then, with his back to the holy man and the prisoner, he showed Lázaro a sheepish smile.

Every question Father Damion asked the prisoner was answered promptly, perhaps even truthfully, as the prisoner avoided looking at the old man. He said: 'I am come here to find what will burn and start fires that others can see.'

Father Damion was skeptical. 'There is little to burn in San Ildefonso.'

The renegade rolled his eyes upwards. 'The cross is wood. It will be the signal.'

Lázaro caught Henriques barely in time, and the prisoner half started up from his bench. Father Damion scowled at the old man. Lázaro assured him: 'I told you he will die. Leave it at that.'

The frightened *guerrillo* remained standing in a crouch.

'And if you don't set the cross afire?' Father Damion asked.

'They will come. It is planned to drive horses from south of here. When the people are upset about that, the men will be able to get into the village from the east and west.'

Father Damion faced Lázaro. They exchanged no words but punched and pushed the prisoner in the direction of the darkened huddle of adobe buildings.

Ghosts were still flitting throughout the village. One woman stopped to watch as the captive was driven down the center of the road. She faded from sight as the men passed. If they had noticed her, neither Lázaro Guardia, the priest, nor the white-headed old man slackened stride.

The light of candles showed from the saloon. Two men, smoking outside, watched the prisoner being driven in their direction. One man dropped his smoke, stepped on it, and went inside. The other man continued to smoke and watch.

When the prisoner was pushed inside, there was not a sound. Juan Bohorquez leaned on his bar top. Torres Mendoza and Rafael Cardinál stood motionless, showing no expression. Father Damion pushed the prisoner into a chair. He and Lázaro exchanged a look. White the rat-eyed prisoner was unknown to them both, there was something in the long silence that suggested that among the defenders the prisoner was not a total stranger.

Rafael Cardinál went to the doorway, pushed outward into the night, and called a woman's name. He had to repeat his call three times before the woman crossed from the west side to the *cantina*.

She and Rafael Cardinál spoke briefly before Rafael stepped close and held one of the spindle doors open. The woman was a shadow outside. She said: '*Sí*, he is the one.'

'You are sure?'

The woman was positive. 'I have slept with closed eyes and have seen his face.'

Rafael jerked his head for the woman to go back to what she was doing, using darkness and mud buildings as concealment while she joined others, watching and waiting. Rafael let the door close at his back. Every man in the saloon gazed at the prisoner who was now sweating.

Juan Bohorquez asked how the renegade had been caught. When it was said that he had been stealing the golden candlesticks off the mission's altar, the one among them who spoke the least, Fulgencio Aramas, the caféman, said: 'Break his bones and throw him on a manure pile.'

There was a murmur of assent. The prisoner spoke hoarsely and rapidly. 'That woman came to me. She wanted me to favor her in my blankets. It was the woman who...'

Rafael Cardinál moved too swiftly for anyone to stop him. It had been his wife outside the doorway who had identified the rapist. He knocked the prisoner from the chair. Lázaro stood up. Only the priest tried to interfere. Lázaro blocked him. The prisoner screamed. Rafael Cardinál's right arm rose and fell four times. When the arm was rising again, Lázaro caught it and swung Rafael away. Father Damion had to hurry, and it was questionable whether his final prayers had been spoken in time.

They dragged the body outside, propped it against a mud wall, and returned to the saloon where Juan Bohorquez solemnly and silently set up several bottles.

Father Damion took Lázaro aside. He wanted to bring the wounded Otero from behind Maria Alvarez's house to the saloon. Lázaro asked the barman for a blanket, which Bohorquez produced, and was dragooned into helping bring the wounded *bandolero* back to the center of the village.

Several men who joined the holy man and *el jefe* gave Maria Alvarez's house a wide berth. There was no general conviction about how she had died, but everyone was aware that *fantasmas,* even *Señor Satán* himself, were busiest at night.

Otero was conscious when they got him onto the blanket and, holding it taut so there was no sag, started back with him. Once he spoke – in English – to the priest. 'I want you to know I came up here only to meet the wagon with guns. They were badly needed by the Mejia revolutionaries... I was against attacking the village.'

Father Damion, keeping stride with the other blanket-bearers, made a dry reply. 'Why did you change your mind?'

'I didn't change it.'

'Then how did you get shot by those defending San Ildefonso?'

'Father, I have no idea who shot me. It was a dark night.'

From the opposite side of the blanket Lázaro Guardia asked a question. 'What is the sense of attacking a small village?'

Joáquin Otero rolled his head and looked steadily at Lázaro. 'Spanish gold. There is said to be a great hoard of it.'

Lázaro's next question was as dry as dead grass. 'Do you believe that, *señor?* Since I was a child, I have heard that story about many places where the Spanish had a camp.'

'Was treasure found at those places?' Otero asked. When Lázaro shook his head, the *gachupín* straightened on the blanket, closed his eyes, and did not speak again until they put him on a pallet at the saloon where feeble candlelight made him look wan to the point of death.

Efraim Montoya crouched beside the pallet with his medicine pouch. As he bared Otero's injuries and turned to ask for two chickens, Flaherty, the freighter, with William at his side came up, asked that a candle be held, and also examined the wounds. Addressing the boy in English, he told him to fetch a basin of clean hot water before turning to the *curandero*. Flaherty was a man who rarely smiled. He addressed the old medicine man in surprisingly accentless Spanish. 'Go, you,

143

tend the others, scrap of soiled pubic hair that you are.'

Efraim Montoya seemed to have been transformed into stone. His scrawny, sinewy, ageless body was completely motionless as he stared at the freighter.

Father Damion touched the *curandero's* shoulder lightly as the man jerked his head. Others in the saloon waited for the explosion they expected. For a brief moment there was absolute silence.

Joáquin Otero opened his eyes. 'Be at peace,' he told the medicine man. 'You have enemies outside, not here inside.'

Montoya unwound off the floor. While doing this, he did not once take his eyes off Patrick Flaherty. He took his medicine bundle with him and, without a sound or a glance at the others, left the *cantina*.

William brought water. Flaherty pushed up his sleeves, rinsed both hands, and asked if the saloonman had a blue bottle. Laudanum came in blue bottles. It was a pointless question. In San Ildefonso there was no laudanum and never had been.

Flaherty told William to wipe the sweat from Otero's face. As this was being done, the grizzled freighter held a candle low as he meticulously examined each wound. When he straightened back, he spoke to Joáquin Otero in Spanish. 'There will be pain. You can faint. It would be a blessing.'

Otero had a question. 'What will you do?'

This was said in English and was answered in the same language. 'Clean you. Get every speck of dust and pieces of your shirt out of the wounds, bandage them. Change the bandages every day. If there is pus, mister, it will come from inside, and nothing I know of can save you.'

Flaherty did as he had told the wounded *gachupín* he intended to do. Men crowded close to watch until Flaherty growled, after which they moved back.

A beetle-browed dark villager, who had been drinking steadily, asked loudly why they were wasting time, doctoring a man who was not only a *gachupín* but also a *bandolero*, the enemy of everyone in San Ildefonso.

Father Damion took the speaker outside, told him to find a place, and stay away from the saloon.

The villager turned on the priest. 'You think God will protect us, Father? God don't know where San Ildefonso is. That *gachupín* on the floor is...'

'Go!'

'And if I don't, Father, the earth will open up and swallow me?'

Father Damion had no chance to reply. A furious fusillade of gunfire erupted at the lower end of the village. The drunk's mouth fell open. He ran for the nearest dark place between buildings. His name was Adolfo

Gutièrrez. Although he had not owned a rosary for twenty years, he remembered the prayer for each bead, thanks to a long dead grandmother who drilled him every night on his knees at bedtime, and now he reeled off each prayer without hesitation where he crouched.

Chapter Ten

The Believers

Within moments the saloon was emptied of men and women. When Lázaro reached the roadway, Father Damion said: 'That filth told the truth. I hear horses.'

Lázaro moved swiftly southward where gunfire was diminishing. He called to the priest to have people go beyond the buildings and watch for infiltrators. The priest turned back as Lázaro heard running horses. Before he reached the rude barricade behind which Isabel Montenegro's female warriors were firing, he had a moment of second thought. Why would invaders, whose lives depended upon their horses, push their animals into a charge at the lower end of town? The answer came about the time Lázaro saw the women behind their barricade – because the invaders meant to take the town, after which they could retrieve their loose horses that had created the diversion.

At the barricade there seemed to be no order. Several animals had been shot before it. Their falling bodies had broken past the makeshift barrier of piled tables, chairs, taut rawhide ropes, and upended bedsteads. Several of the terrified horses had jumped the barricade and raced blindly up the roadway. The marauders were close behind the horses. Lázaro could hear their shouts. So could the rifle-firing women. They aimed in the direction of the shouting.

It was impossible, for as long as the pandemonium lasted, to ascertain casualties. Lázaro aimed twice at shadows, and both times the targets vanished in the darkness and smoke.

A woman screamed. The sound was drowned by rattling gunfire. Lázaro went in the direction of the scream. The *guerrilleros* were now firing. Bits and pieces of wood flew in all directions. The invaders pushed their attack with unrelenting force. Gunfire was deafening. Gunsmoke was thick. If Isabel Montenegro had drilled her *amazonas*, the fight showed no indication of it. But the one thing she had told them, they did: they fought like tigers, yielding only when protective parts of their barricade were blown away.

A man, loudly cursing in English, caught and held Lázaro's attention. Flaherty was angrily yelling at William beside him to lie flat and stay down. The lad had a rifle that he reloaded as Lázaro watched, rose to a kneeling position, took long aim, and fired. The recoil knocked him flat. Flaherty landed atop William, yelling for him to stay down.

Lázaro's shield was a massive oaken table that might slow bullets but would not prevent them from penetrating. He ducked when a long sliver was torn loose. As he straightened up to seek whoever was using a rifle, Isabel Montenegro appeared beside him. She gasped: 'There are too many.' Lázaro ignored her to seek a target. She jostled his arm. 'We need the cannon.'

He looked around. Isabel Montenegro looked back, hair straggling, sweaty face streaked with smudges of dirt. Lázaro silently agreed. He should have thought of that. The cannon would have decimated the invaders. It was in the alley on the east side of town. It required ten strong men to move it.

He sank down with his back to the oak table. 'What we need,' he loudly told her, 'is soldiers. Lots of them.'

Isabel Montenegro spat in disgust. The *norteamericanos* were at their fort a hard day's ride from San Ildefonso.

The gunfire slackened to a ragged occasional fusillade as Lázaro got up on his knees to peek around the table. When he turned back, he told Isabel their enemies had achieved their purpose and would now be sneaking into the village behind them. Isabel ignored the occasional gunshots. She said: 'Not all of them, *jefe*.'

Lázaro left her behind the old table. There

was an occasional gunshot among the buildings northward. The rapist Rafael Cardinál had killed had been right. Following the charge of riderless horses against the southern barricade – a desperate diversion – the marauders were now getting among the buildings. The gunshots he heard as he went northward were probably not invaders being shot, but unsuspecting villagers.

Torres Mendoza stepped from a dark dogtrot to say that the drunken Adolfo Gutièrrez, whom Father Damion had taken out of the saloon, now lay dead between two buildings. 'Shot in the back.' Lázaro nodded. The drunk had had the misfortune to be in a narrow dark place when an infiltrating raider had found him.

There was no light showing from the *cantina*. Only one building still showed light, and it was too feeble and too distant to be noticeable. Someone at the mission had lighted several candles.

Lázaro and Torres Mendoza went to the nearest *pasadizo,* the same one where the drunk had been shot. It was not possible to make sense of the fighting. Even if it had been daylight, it would have been difficult to determine who among the *jacales* was an enemy and who a friend.

They stealthily made their way along the east side as far as the *cantina* and announced themselves at the door. Inside, the wounded were sitting, some in chairs, others on the floor with their backs to the wall, watching the roadway doors. They were all armed. Lázaro prayed that no villager would come in unexpectedly from the roadway. With the light of only one candle on the bar, killing a friend would be as easy as killing an enemy.

Lázaro groped his way to a particular pallet and sank to one knee. Joáquin Otero looked up. 'It sounds like a battle,' he said.

Lázaro nodded. 'It is a battle, *señor*. How many are there?'

'*¿Quión sabe?* After all the shooting...?'

'How many were there, then?'

'Three bands ... in total maybe sixty.'

'How many people are there in San Ildefonso?'

'To fight? Maybe the same number, but as many women with weapons as men.'

'Thirty men to fight.' Joáquin Otero sighed. 'I would like a drink from the bar.'

Lázaro had become accustomed to gunfire and ignored it as he got a bottle and returned with it. There were others who were wounded and waiting to fight again. Their interest remained exclusively on the roadway door. As Lázaro handed over the bottle, the only glass window in Juan Bohorquez's saloon exploded inward into splinters. None of the waiting injured commented, but replacing that glass would cost a small fortune.

Joáquin Otero swallowed three times and

151

handed back the bottle. Because Lázaro did not take a drink, Otero shrugged and watched as Lázaro placed the bottle to one side. 'For once I wish the *yanqui* soldiers would come,' the *gachupín* said. 'They take prisoners. The Mexicans don't.'

A woman came in, put her back to the doors, and, crouching slightly, caught the attention of those inside. She held her rifle low in both hands. In poor light it was difficult to identify her, but, when she faced around, only Joáquin Otero did not recognize Isabel Montenegro. She saw Lázaro and called to him. 'They are in among us.' Lázaro nodded. By now everyone knew that. But what else she said made his eyes widen. 'They are working their way toward the mission. Some of them, anyway.'

Lázaro got to his feet, briefly hesitated, then followed Isabel Montenegro back out into the night, where the moon was gone, and a faint chill had taken its place. Dawn was not far off. Up until now the villagers had held their own.

When they were outside, Isabel said: 'Tomás Henriques is in the bell tower. It is possible to see flashes of his rifle. If we can make them all go up there...'

'That,' stated Lázaro Guardia, 'is why they are here.' Before the woman could ask questions, Lázaro told her to go back to the saloon and find Torres Mendoza and, if possible, Juan Bohorquez and any others who were able, and tell them to go to the mission.

Isabel Montenegro stood, staring. 'And strip the village of defenders when we are already chasing them away?'

Lázaro said: 'Yes. Go!'

The woman went but carried with her a strong measure of disagreement.

Her husband, José, was on the east side sitting in darkness with the cannon when Lázaro found him. José looked up. 'It is murder,' he said. 'Friends shooting friends.'

Lázaro told the gunner to find enough men to help him drag the gun to the north end of town. 'Fill it with whatever you can find.'

José did not get to his feet, but he stared. 'They are together up there, then?'

'José, get your cannon up there. It would help if we had cannon balls, but there must be something ... what did you load it with the last time?'

A pronounced shrug preceded the reply. 'Scraps of iron, horseshoes, and muleshoes, spikes, whatever of iron or steel could be found. Why would cannon balls be better?'

Lázaro did not explain. 'Get some help and move the gun to the north end of town.

'How can I get anyone to...?'

'José, *do it!* I think we have this one chance to stay alive.'

For the gunner locating men to help with

153

the cannon was a perilous business. Sniping was continuous on both sides of the dusty roadway.

Lázaro hunted up the priest, found him hunkering with three older men and two women. They were concentrating on the Cardinál house. The priest explained that several enemies were over there. Lázaro took the priest behind Morisco's store. 'Otero told me he thought they would concentrate on the mission.'

Father Damion made a rueful smile. 'The Spanish cache ... of a certainty.'

'Father, José Montenegro is getting men to help him drag the cannon to the north end of town.'

The priest noticeably stiffened. 'You will bombard the mission?'

'Do you think they will surrender?'

'But Lázaro, it has stood almost two hundred years. In better times, when there was trade, the mission of San Ildefonso was the only place for hundreds of miles where...!'

'Father, I want to do this even less than you do. If we don't beat them, *zopilotes* will eat our carcasses. If the Lord will put them all in one place, we might survive.'

The priest looked northward. From the east side, behind buildings, he could see the old mission with its cross askew and its fine bell tower. He thought of something. 'What about Tomás Henriques, Lázaro.'

154

If there was an answer, Lázaro did not have it. 'We can shout to him to leave, and they will shoot him as he runs.'

'Lázaro, there is something you don't know, and which I can't tell you. What's said in the confessional nave cannot be repeated.'

Lázaro nodded. He knew this, and, while he wondered what secret only Tomás Henriques and the priest shared, his fundamental concern had to do with something else.

Behind them men were straining with ropes to move the cannon. José had succeeded. Lázaro wondered what José had told them to get them to move the big gun.

Father Damion walked away, mindless of the sniping. Lázaro went to help with the cannon. Twice he and the others were shouted at from snipers' places of concealment. The last time it was a woman who called. It was the angular Indian whose daughter had given birth with Isabel Montenegro's son at her side. Whatever the Indian woman said none of the men understood, but they did understand her hand gestures and smiled as they strained and grunted.

The Indian woman had a rifle. Somewhere she had found a Winchester saddle gun, no good for long-range killing, but ideal for the kind of fighting that was done among buildings in a village.

Whoever owned that bugle overrode all other sounds with a long, trilling blast. For

155

several moments the sniping gunfire stopped. Some of the *guerrilleros* called out that soldiers were coming, which was what the bugle had told those who had been soldiers in Old Mexico. When no soldiers appeared, the sniping became brisk again.

It was not just hot – it was swelteringly hot. The men with the cannon broke away, one or two at a time, to find water to drink and to fill hats to douse themselves with.

Inherent in Mexicans on both sides of the border was an urge to call out either jokes or insults. As José's helpers struggled, they berated each other, made jokes about those working hardest, calling them sons of a brass monkey. For Lázaro Guardia, with the last *jacal* in sight, he called out that they urgently required a miracle. Sweat-soaked old men called back that while the good Lord was merciful – when it suited Him to be – He was unbelievably stingy with miracles.

When they had the cannon behind the last house where there was thin shade, a stalwart villager named Genero Salas straightened up slowly, looking to the northeast as he said: 'Lázaro. What is it? There is nothing but the church out there.' The man turned to gaze steadily at Lázaro. 'What is this for? That is the house of God.'

The other men squinted through sweat-drenched eyes. They seemed to have taken root. Lázaro told them to go back and join the snipers. Some went but Genero Salas did not move. 'You aren't going to do this,' he told Lázaro. 'Why? The *bandoleros* are at the village, not over there.'

Lázaro told the indignant villager to come with him. He led the way back to the middle of the village. Salas remained wary. Where they paused for water, he eyed Lázaro skeptically. 'You will leave the cannon up there for only old Henriques in his bell tower to see?'

'No,' Lázaro replied. 'The brigands are moving northward as they fight, sniping from house to house as they go.'

The older man had noticed no such thing. He cocked his head. 'Listen, does that sound like they are not fighting in San Ildefonso?'

Lázaro heard Juan Bohorquez behind him and turned. Bohorquez was neither blind nor insensate. He screwed up his face. '*¿Amigos, qué paso?*'

The older man spoke first. 'He has had the cannon pulled northward to bombard the mission.'

Bohorquez's frown tightened. 'Lázaro...?'

The priest appeared unannounced. Salas repeated what he had told Juan Bohorquez. Lázaro stood mutely, watching Father Damion. The priest began to address the stalwart man, eye to eye: 'Genero...'

'Father, for two hundred years my family has been baptized there. Among the graves are my forefathers. What Lázaro wants to do is sacrilege.'

As though all this had not been said, the priest started over. 'Genero, what damage happens we will repair.'

'Father, you agree with this?'

'No, but I want to see you, your wife, and four little girls in the church, maybe not next Sabbath but the one after.'

Salas looked steadily at the priest, then at Lázaro Guardia, ignored several bystanders, and walked stiffly away. As he passed between two houses, a bullet chipped adobe from a wall he had just passed. He neither ducked for cover nor flinched.

Father Damion said: 'He has served the altar since he was a child.'

The sniping began to have ragged interludes of silence. Several of the attackers called taunts. They were answered as often as not by women.

Father Damion went northward where he threw an old wagon canvas over the little cannon. When the insults and sniping both increased, he went carefully down the east side where there were more defenders than attackers, found Lázaro still there, and grudgingly agreed that he was right: the attackers were working their way toward the mission. He also said: 'If what they wanted was to ransack the mission for treasure, why did they attack San Ildefonso?'

Lázaro's reply was succinct. 'You will have to ask them, Father.'

Moses Morisco had closed the steel shutters over his roadway window much earlier. By mid-afternoon they were faintly scarred from bullets. Morisco hunted for every bullet in his store and handed them to those who came to the store. He remained inside except for one brief trip to his shed. When he returned, he considered several places to hide sticks of dynamite where they would be unlikely to be found. There were enough of those sticks that, if they were detonated, San Ildefonso would be leveled.

As afternoon wore along, the attackers seemed to increase their northward progress. By early dusk there were only a few attackers left to engage the villagers. Juan Bohorquez said he thought that was deliberate. If the defenders could be kept among the *jacales,* it would provide time for the raiders to search for treasure. Bohorquez, like Lázaro Guardia and others, was skeptical of the existence of any hidden wealth. Every clutch of old adobe houses near a mission had tales of buried treasure. He told Rafael Cardinál it interested him to wonder why, if the old-time Spaniards had accumulated great stores of gold, they hadn't taken it with them when they left. Rafael Cardinál had no answer.

As dusk settled, the gunfire became occasional and ragged. As with the previous night people went to the saloon. The wounded there were fed, not very well, but as well as could be when women dared not go to their homes for fear brigands were waiting.

Pat Flaherty and the undersized William sat apart. Flaherty ate sparingly and made a point of seeing that William ate his fill. It was a unique partnership, the abandoned child and the grizzled freighter, neither of whom had been completely accepted by the villagers until the fighting had started.

Lázaro Guardia and Juan Bohorquez stealthily rummaged the open area between the village and the mission. When they were able to hear voices, they blended into the increasing dusk, belly-down, and listened. It was probably the nearness of their objective that made the attackers argumentative. Lázaro wondered about Tomás Henriques in the loft. Searchers would certainly find him. On the other hand, if anyone knew a place of concealment, it had to be Henriques who had lived at the mission for years.

Juan Bohorquez nudged his companion. 'If they can be got together outside...?'

Lázaro asked about the mission candle-sticks. Juan last remembered seeing them in his saloon. 'Why?' he asked. 'They will find candles in the church.'

'Because, if they found golden candlesticks outside, they might all go to that place. The candlesticks are gold. They want gold.'

'And how do the candlesticks get over here for them to find?'

'If you will go back and bring them to me, I'll do the rest.'

Juan Bohorquez raised his head, stared briefly before beginning to crawl backward until it was safe to rise and return to the village. On the way he encountered Genero Salas who was still adamantly against using the cannon. Salas returned to the saloon with Bohorquez. He was of the opinion no one could reach the mission as long as the plunderers were making their search.

Juan agreed but not out loud. He found the candlesticks and started back, indifferent whether his acquaintance came or not. Salas followed without being asked.

Their abrupt appearance at the saloon had caught and held the attention of the wounded, those who were caring for them, and others. They had said nothing as they got the candlesticks and ventured back out into the night. Moments after their departure someone said they should be followed. Whatever they were up to, golden candlesticks did not grow on trees.

It was Father Damion who discouraged this. Clearly, if the mission priest did not fear theft, the others, while still fearing it, would

161

hesitate to follow the thieves. It was Efraim Montoya, kneeling beside a wounded villager, who sharply said: 'Maybe they will give the candlesticks to the *guerrilleros* in exchange for our lives. They wouldn't steal them ... not *el jefe* or Genero Salas who prays three times a day.'

The *curandero* was right to some degree. When Bohorquez and his companion located Lázaro Guardia and gave him the candlesticks, he had used the half hour of waiting to perfect an idea. He told Bohorquez and Salas to remain where they were, to be prepared to shoot only if Lázaro were detected or captured, then he left them, crawling like a lizard until they could no longer see him.

What Lázaro had in mind was not to place the candlesticks where they would not be too easily discovered. This thought had convinced him the graveyard should be his objective. The invaders had built a small fire on the east side of the mission. The villagers could see it but not well enough to discern men near it because of the long roofed-over gallery along the east wall that added its gloominess to the night. But this created a problem for Lázaro whose destination was the graveyard. He had to waste an entire hour crawling and creeping far enough to the east to be invisible to the men at the fire who were making a meal of what they had

162

ransacked from the mission.

The invaders were loud and argumentative. It seemed that each one of them had his own opinion where the treasure was hidden. During their discussion they ate, drank mission wine, and kept the fire fed as Lázaro crept ahead, inches at a time. When he was close enough to feel heat, he searched for an old stone grave marker that was askew, dug with both hands, put the candlesticks in the small trench, and sprinkled dirt over all but the upper ends.

He then began crawling back and encountered his first peril. A renegade, who had taken on more than his share of mission wine, came unsteadily among the grave markers to urinate. Where he finally halted, Lázaro was less than twenty feet distant behind a pair of markers of a man and his wife whose wish that they be buried side by side had been granted.

The unwashed marauder decided to urinate on the marker Lázaro had used to conceal the candlesticks. He was unsteady on his feet. He considered other gravestones, looked up at the heavens, and eventually looked down.

For ten seconds he did not move, and, when he did, he used one foot to scrape aside moist earth. He leaned farther over, carefully brushed more earth aside, and softly said: *'Madre de Dios.'* Then he let go with a yell loud enough to be heard in the village.

Men came running. Lázaro crawled as fast as he could before getting to his feet and running harder than he had ever run before. They should have seen him. He expected them to, but what the micturating raider had found – two partially buried golden candlesticks – caused noisy excitement. One bull-brassed renegade yelled: 'I knew it. It would be among the graves because people do not dig among the dead. I knew it would be out here!'

Lázaro led the way back to the village where several people wanted to know what had happened. They had heard the yell. People emerged like wraiths from among the *jacales,* about equal parts of both sexes. Isabel Montenegro arrived with several of her *amazonas.*

Juan Bohorquez, not normally a praying man, crossed himself. 'It was God's mercy!' he exclaimed. 'They should have seen Lázaro when he ran.'

Chapter Eleven

Waiting

The agitated marauders in the mission grave-yard were alternately cursing, calling for digging implements, and going among head-stones, kicking some and clawing with bare hands at others. There was no moon, but there was residual heat from the day. Flaherty arrived, having survived a prolonged duel with an invader who had broken away when he heard the yell from the north. William was with him, carrying a rifle taller than he was. During the excitement the boy went to the front of the cannon, reached in, withdrew a hand, and said: 'Fire it! What are you waiting for? They are bunched together over there.'

José Montenegro was lighting the linstock when the stalwart Genero Salas stuck the lighted stick aside and glared. José was too startled to retrieve the firing stick. Salas said: 'You would desecrate the graves?'

Lázaro looked for Father Damion, did not see him, and approached the indignant man. 'The gun is aimed high enough to miss the gravestones. Look, you, this chance will not come again!'

Salas turned a smoldering glare on Guardia. 'My mother is buried there ... may God bless her ... and my father. Even my grandfather and his father.'

'José, tell him how the cannon is aimed.'

Isabel's husband did not get the chance to speak. Torres Mendoza, agitated and angry, braced the stalwart man. 'So are my parents buried there. And my grandparents and a sister I never knew because she was born dead. *We* are alive. The dead know nothing. Genero, be sensible.'

Salas glared. 'It is sacrilege,' he said again. 'The bones will be torn from the earth and scattered.'

The freighter moved close and swung his right arm overhead and down. Genero Salas collapsed in a heap. The shock held everyone around the gun like statues. Flaherty did not raise his voice as he said: 'Drag him out of the way. William, get me that smoking stick.'

But the cannon was not fired. The renegades became exhausted from furious, indiscriminate digging. The man with the foghorn voice said they needed daylight and led the way back inside the mission where cobweb-encrusted bottles of wine were again passed around.

Lázaro's companions with the cannon relaxed a little at a time. One woman was looking down when she said: 'Genero is a fool. He made us waste time. Now the chance has gone.'

The few remaining snipers, probably after hearing the exultant cries from the mission, used darkness to advantage by abandoning the village and making their way to the old church. This was not certain until a number of hair-triggered villagers went from house to house. They found only one man, not a renegade, a very old villager whose throat had been cut. There was blood everywhere. They covered him and continued their search without finding a single renegade. Eventually they returned to the *cantina* to report the result of their search.

Isabel Montenegro and Francesca Cardinál led a party of *amazonas* among the houses. All they found, excepting the murdered old man under his blanket, was broken furniture, empty cupboards, and general destruction. They gathered what food they could find and returned to the saloon with it.

Juan Bohorquez went along to the store to appeal to Moses Morisco and nearly got himself shot. The storekeeper, who had barred his roadside door and whose front window was still covered, had not dropped the *tranca* into its hangers on his rear door. When Juan entered in almost total darkness, someone cocked a pistol.

Juan dropped flat as he called out. 'Storekeeper, it is I, Juan Bohorquez.'

It seemed an eternity before a ghost walked toward the rear door and said: 'Stand up.'

Juan rose. He and the storekeeper faced one another over a scant ten feet.

Morisco turned slightly aside, eased down the dog of his dragoon revolver, and turned back. 'What is the situation, Juan?'

Bohorquez related what he knew, even mentioning Genero Salas's refusal to allow the cannon to be fired.

The storekeeper said: 'And they are gathered at the saloon?'

'Yes.'

'Wait here.'

Juan waited until the man returned and handed him three sticks of dynamite wrapped in their red waxed paper. Juan frowned as he took the explosives. 'We are out of food at the *cantina*. We have the wounded up there.'

Morisco put aside the horse pistol and made a wide gesture with both arms. 'Help yourself. I will get the medicine box. Go, then. Do as I said. Help yourself.'

Bohorquez went among the shelves, filling his shirt until he found a large knit shopping bag after which he used that. When it became very heavy and he had slung it over his shoulder, Morisco said: 'Wait. I will help you.' He also went among the shelves.

When they were ready, Juan Bohorquez led the way, warily and without haste. When they reached the rear of his saloon, he used a pistol butt to hammer loudly. When the door was opened, there were three cocked pistols and one full-sized rifle at rest atop a wooden crate where a deadly serious urchin cocked it.

Moses Morisco entered last. He was bowed under the weight of his burden until the freighter appeared to relieve him. By candlelight the storekeeper looked like an ancient prophet, the one holding the graven tablets. The food was given to the women. The saloon had a wood stove that had only two burners. Women crowded around it. Very little was said. Morisco found a stool, sat, and solemnly regarded the injured, including the light-complected one named Otero.

He wanted to know what the defenders intended to do come daylight, and Flaherty told him. 'They are at the mission. When they come out, we've got the cannon waiting.'

Morisco studied Flaherty. He and the freighter were the only *gringos*. 'There was a stronghold called Masada,' he said, speaking softly. 'It was besieged by enemies who outnumbered the defenders. I have heard that story a dozen times, and I always wondered why the defenders didn't sneak down in the darkness and kill their besiegers.'

Torres Mendoza was interested. 'Why

didn't they?'

'I don't know. All I know is that they all died on their hilltop.'

One of the women had a question for the storekeeper. 'You are saying, then, that we should sneak up to the mission in the dark?'

Morisco accepted the coffee someone offered and made a delayed reply. 'Can it be done? Isn't it better to try than to crouch in here like the people of Masada until it is too late?'

Food was passed around, mostly cold because it all could not be heated quickly enough on only two burners. While people ate, there was silence. The idea of abandoning the village to try and reach the mission undetected held a definite certainty of risk. It was very likely the renegades over there would have watchers. Drinking mission wine would possibly make some of them sleep like stones, but not all, and those *guerrilleros* were experienced raiders. Without a doubt surprising them, drunk or sober, would result in casualties.

Pat Flaherty sat with the small boy, eating, listening, and occasionally wagging his head. A woman, annoyed by this, turned on the freighter. 'You have a better idea, *Fletar?*'

'Only one, *señora*. You saw how crazy they acted in the graveyard. You saw them quit and go into the mission. In the morning with good light they will go back to dig among the graves. Broad daylight will be better than last night, when there was an argument about firing the gun.

After the freighter finished speaking, silence settled again, but this time there was a difference. It had nothing to do with eating everything in sight.

Father Damion came in out of the night. People looked up but said nothing. The priest went to Joáquin Otero's pallet and knelt. He studied the ailing *gachupín* a long moment before asking a question. 'Those Mexicans, *señor*. Were they chased over the line by *Federales*, or did they come for another reason?'

Otero had dark circles under each eye. When he answered, his voice echoed tiredness. 'What I can tell you is that I was serving the *pronunciados* in a good cause, to overthrow a rotten government. I only met the *guerrilleros* after I returned.'

'And you joined them?'

'Why do you ask these questions? What is it you want to know?'

The priest reached under his upper garment, brought forth a scrap of crumpled and soiled cloth, and flattened it, using both hands. He and the *gachupín* lowered their eyes. After a moment Otero asked where the priest had got the cloth map, and Father Damion replied while tucking the soiled cloth back in a pocket. 'It was inside the lining of your brother's *alforjas*. The people who cared for him, until he died, found it.'

'And they gave it to you?'

'No. They gave it to Maria Alvarez. She used it for a handkerchief. I found it when I was preparing her for burial. What does the old map look like to you with those marks?' Father Damion did not await an answer. He leaned forward as he spoke again. 'The mission is clearly marked. The only written words mean *it is here*.'

Otero's eyes briefly brightened. 'My brother showed it to me. That's why I joined the *bandoleros*. To find what is on the map.'

Father Damion, who had studied the cloth carefully and over a long period of time, said: '*Señor*, have you ever been to the Mission San Luis Rey in a small place called Santa Rosa, southeast of Albuquerque, on the Pecos River?'

'No.'

'You're certain?'

'I have never been as far north as Albuquerque.'

'*Señor*, this map can be overlaid on a map of the San Luis Rey country and its missions, and everything fits perfectly.'

Joáquin Otero stared in silence for almost a full minute before speaking. 'It was my brother's map. He said we should get the *guerrilleros* to attack San Ildefonso.'

'Why would he want that done when the

172

Spanish cache is up north?' Otero looked away without speaking, so Father Damion answered for him. 'To make the *guerrilleros* think the cache was here, and the two of you could find the cache at San Luis Rey?'

Joáquin Otero flushed red.

Someone spoke from behind the priest. Pat Flaherty knelt to examine the bandaging and wrinkled his nose. Father Damion instinctively leaned farther back. The freighter jerked his head. He and the priest moved to a dark corner where the freighter said: 'One more day. Maybe two or three, but no more than three.'

Otero feebly signaled for the holy man to return, which Father Damion did. Otero said: 'The map shows a road going southward toward San Ildefonso.'

The priest gently shook his head. 'That's not a road, that is the Pecos River. Is there a river east of here? Not for many miles, my friend. There is a road but not as it is drawn on the map. It bends and turns, following cañons until it reaches San Ildefonso. It lies many miles west of the river.' At the expression on the wounded man's face Father Damion said the last words he would ever speak to Joáquin Otero, the *gachupín*. '*Señor*, ten years ago a cache was found in the walls of San Luis Rey Mission while repairs were being made.'

Otero's eyes held steadily on the holy

man's face. 'Then I will die for nothing.'

Father Damion did not answer. He went to the bar where men were talking without much spirit. One woman, a sturdy individual with straggling black hair, armed with a pistol and a huge fleshing knife, pushed a bottle toward the priest as she spoke. 'What about the old man in the bell tower?'

'Well, what of Tomás Henriques?' the priest replied, ignoring the bottle.

'When they find him, they will torture him.'

'If they find him, *señora*, it will be a miracle. Tomás Henriques has haunted the church longer than I have been here. He has shown me places no one knew about.'

Juan Bohorquez took the priest aside and showed him the sticks of dynamite. The priest rolled his eyes. 'They could blow us all to pieces of meat. What are you going to do with them?'

'Wait until very early in the morning before sunrise, crawl to the church, light one stick and pitch it inside while they are sleeping.'

'It will destroy the mission, Juan.'

'Father, you have said yourself that, if we don't kill them, they will kill us.'

'Leave it to the cannon, Juan.'

'And if that doesn't do it?'

Father Damion smiled tiredly and walked away.

Efraim Montoya approached the holy

man. 'The *gachupín* should be killed, Father.'

'In God's good time, Efraim.'

'Maybe we could ransom him to those *hombres malas.*'

The priest considered the elfin *curandero*. 'They wouldn't pay a *centavo* for him.'

'You can't be sure. We could try. We are desperate people.'

'No. Leave the *gachupín* where he is.'

'We can't offer a trade if he is dead.'

The priest's normally patient and tolerant nature briefly deserted him. He tapped Efraim Montoya over the heart with a rigid finger. 'Leave him be! Stay away from him!'

Several more candles were lighted because some villagers had stealthily gone among the buildings. There were candles but no renegades. When this information was brought to the *cantina*, it confirmed the suspicion that all the renegades were at the mission.

Lázaro was marginally less tired after eating. He and the freighter sat in a murky corner. The urchin was close to Flaherty, holding his rifle upright. The tip of the muzzle was about a foot and a half above his head.

Flaherty had already said what he thought – wait until the diggers were all together in the cemetery, then fire the cannon. If there was another way to make the odds more equal, Pat Flaherty had no idea what it could be, and he had heard all the schemes ad-

175

vanced in the saloon including the *curandero's* suggestion, and in his opinion none deserved consideration. He told Lázaro it was customary with soldiers to be in position so that, when a cannon was fired and its targets were dead or in disarray, soldiers would charge and finish those who were left.

Lázaro sought Isabel Montenegro to repeat what the freighter had said. Her reply was that, as soon as the chill arrived, she would take her *amazonas* northward to be ready. She also told Lázaro that her husband should never have joined the others at the saloon, and Lázaro turned to seek José. He was sitting on the floor with a bottle at his side.

Flaherty knew about loading and firing a cannon. Lázaro returned to him to explain about José, and the freighter nodded. He had been watching the gunner. He agreed to fire the cannon. Before Lázaro walked away, Flaherty said: '*Un momento, jefe.* There is something else. Crazy as those bastards will be to find the cache, remember, those are experienced men. They know we are here. They will expect us to do something, which means none of us here will be able to simply walk over there to fight. They will have watchers out.'

Lázaro went to the roadway door, tested the darkness, was craning northward when Juan Bohorquez came up to mention the sticks of dynamite. Lázaro took down a breath and expelled it before saying: 'If Genero Salas knew this, he would want to take the dynamite from you.'

Bohorquez snorted. 'Genero Salas will have broken bones if he tries it. Do you want me to sneak as close as I can get and throw dynamite inside where the *guerrilleros* are sleeping?'

'They'll have watchers waiting. Juan, if the cannon doesn't do what we want done, then we can use your dynamite.'

'But, Lázaro...'

'There is another reason, Juan. An explosion of dynamite inside the mission will destroy it.'

Bohorquez sneered. 'The priest!'

'No, friend, not the priest. A brave old man is hiding somewhere over there.'

The saloonman's expression changed. He left the doorway and went back behind the bar.

Some of the villagers had slept. Some had sat glumly with unpleasant thoughts. A number of their friends had been wounded. Fewer had been killed. Whatever dawn light brought, the fight to come would be fought over open ground. Those morose souls kept the priest busy. Death could best be faced with a cleansed soul.

The last of the food was eaten. Juan

Bohorquez removed the bottles and put them under the bar on a shelf. Except for José Montenegro and one or two of the older men, none of the defenders was truly drunk.

In after years this night would be remembered as the longest people recalled.

Lázaro returned to the roadway twice. The last time he saw faintly fading stars and smelled the mildly acrid desert night. Dawn was on the way.

He went inside to make an announcement that held no surprises for his companions, except for several details, particularly the one about Isabel Montenegro's female defenders leaving while it was still dark in order to be in position when visibility improved.

Pat Flaherty also left. At the door he asked Lázaro to mind William. Before Lázaro could respond, the boy yanked fiercely on Flaherty's trouser leg and adamantly shook his head without saying a word.

The men watched the boy walk to the roadway and face them, finally speaking: 'They killed *Señor* Lopez who was my only friend.'

Flaherty glanced at Lázaro, rolled his eyes, went over to put a hand on the lad's shoulder. The two in tandem then used the protection of the buildings, conceivably an unnecessary precaution since there had

178

been no sniping since about dusk the night before. Several injured villagers volunteered to join the *amazonas*. Lázaro refused to permit this. Father Damion slipped away while this argument was in progress.

José Montenegro, having been helped to his feet and bracing himself against the bar, had announced he was the only gunner, to which one of the wounded men dryly said that, since it did not require genius to touch a match to a protruding fuse, José would do better if he held down the floor of the saloon which had been disturbed many times by tremors in the earth where the devil lived. José solemnly considered this as his knees gradually gave way, and he slid slowly downward.

There was a faint graying of the world beyond the saloon's spindle doors, and with it came the dawn light's desert fragrance. Men looked to their weapons. Most were old, and using weapons against those who threatened them was not a novelty. They talked a little as each man made sure of the reliability of his weapons. When they were ready to leave the saloon, Juan Bohorquez made one last appeal to Lázaro to use the dynamite.

Father Damion stood stock still, gazing at the saloonman. 'Where did you get dynamite?' he asked.

'From Moses Morisco.'

'How much?'

'Three sticks.'

'Where are they?'

'Under the bar. Why?'

'Give them to me.'

'Why should I do that, Father?'

The priest went behind the bar, found the explosives in their wax paper wrapping, broke each stick, and dropped them into the large tub where Bohorquez washed glasses. They immediately colored the greasy water a dun-brown color.

Father Damion nodded to Lázaro. It was time to fire the cannon – an act that now depended only on how long the marauders slept.

Chapter Twelve

It Is Finished

The mission stood bathed in pale grayness as it had for several hundred years, and, although no one noticed because visibility was not that good, the ocotillo cross atop the bell tower had been straightened. The soiled wagon canvas which covered the cannon was still in place. Isabel Montenegro's defenders had been joined by other women and Francesca Cardinál. They had slight cover from the gun on its heavy sled.

Isabel told them to get down flat, and, as this was done, a hatless, unkempt man left the mission in back, crossed among the graves to urinate, and one of the waiting woman addressed Pat Flaherty without taking her eyes off the distant marauder. 'Listen you, mule man, I offer a wager. Three *yanqui* silver dollars that I can shoot it off from here.'

Flaherty leaned across the cannon to see which woman had made this offer, saw her looking up at him, and said: 'Anyone can hit a man's head from here.'

The woman's answer was crisp. 'Not his head, his *chingadaro*.'

There was a ripple of suppressed laughter. Pat Flaherty turned his back and after a few moments would only face in the direction of the mission. He was red to the hairline.

The renegade went back inside after casting one careless glance in the direction of the village. If the big gun had not been covered, and if the sun had been rising, it would have dazzlingly reflected off the cannon.

There would be no appreciable sunlight for another hour. Lying on *caliche* was uncomfortable any time, but a seemingly endless variety of crawling and biting creatures that lived in this God-forsaken country made life miserable for the defenders, awaiting sunrise. When it came, finally, men crossed from the shade of the long porch on the east side of the mission. When they left shade provided by the overhang, daylight defined them. They were carrying tools. Pat Flaherty stood ready to light the firing match, but he did not light it. 'That's only about half of them.'

Agitated, Juan Bohorquez hissed: 'Fire it. We'll take care of the others. *Gawd dammit, gringo, fire the cannon!*'

Flaherty took his time getting the linstock alight. Before applying it to the fuse, he looked around. People with hands over their ears stood with their backs to the cannon. Flaherty growled at several people directly behind the gun. 'Move away, to one side!' The people moved, and Flaherty applied the burning stick. When the fuse sputtered, Flaherty moved swiftly aside and covered his ears.

The explosion was deafening even to those who had covered their ears. A great gout of smoke concealed people, the gun, even Lázaro Guardia who was far to the east. Men screamed, a few ran, some hobbled, using digging tools as crutches. Several of the prone women made out moving figures and fired at them.

Everything that happened, excepting for the echoes, was over within moments. Lázaro tried to count the bodies among the grave markers. Torres Mendoza came up and said a number in an awed voice. 'Eleven not moving, six moving but unable to stand up.'

Flaherty leaned on the cannon that had made its customary backward recoil a good ten feet from where it had been fired. William sank to the ground. It was the first cannon he had ever seen. As long as he lived, he would remember what it did when it was fired.

Several women kept up their rifle fire even after Lázaro could no longer see fleeing marauders. Isabel Montenegro called sharply for them to save bullets, and the firing ceased.

Juan Bohorquez approached Lázaro Guardia and Torres Mendoza who were standing together. He addressed Lázaro. 'Now I can run past the chapel doors and throw in a stick

183

of dynamite.'

Lázaro had no opportunity to speak. Father Damion was behind the saloonman when he said: 'You will do no such thing.'

Bohorquez swung around, wild-eyed and sweating. 'The cannon got maybe half. One stick of dynamite will finish them.'

'They are finished,' the priest said. 'If you want to risk your life, take a white cloth, and walk up there, yelling for them to surrender.'

Juan Bohorquez was clearly excited, but he was not stupid. He said: 'You take the white rag, *Padre*. My mother did not raise any fools.'

'Maybe one,' the priest retorted and moved past where Lázaro was standing. 'It was your idea, Juan, and it was a good idea, but now we have many graves to dig.'

Someone was sniping from one of the high, barred windows of the chapel. Isabel took the women farther back, grouping them for protection behind the cannon.

More than one sniper fired. Lázaro and Father Damion counted muzzle blasts. Lázaro said: 'Three.'

The holy man said: 'Four.'

The sun climbed. Most of the defenders trickled back to the village where it would be cool, and where there was water. Torres Mendoza nudged Lázaro and jutted his jaw. The last of the *amazonas* to leave was the tall, angular Indian woman carrying the Winchester carbine. Lázaro, the priest, Torres Mendoza, and one or two others lingered near the cannon, making use of what cover the big gun provided.

Torres Mendoza said: 'Now, we wait until dark. I think there are more of us than there are of them.'

No one commented, but the holy man spoke quietly while gazing at the mission. 'They will have wounded men, dying men maybe.'

No one commented about that either, and a half hour later, when the sniping ceased, they trudged back to the village and the saloon.

Efraim Montoya said they should drag the dead *gachupín* outside. Shortly now the corpse would become offensive. Otero was removed from the saloon. The other dead man, Alfredo Lopez, was swelling under his soiled canvas covering. There would be others, not to mention dead horses. Something had to be done and soon, but the graveyard was untenable. It also had dead bodies, lying in the heat and sunlight.

Juan Bohorquez went among the northernmost structures to spy on the mission. When he returned, he startled everyone with an announcement. 'They have a white sheet on the end of a shepherd's crook, sticking out of the door.'

The freighter broke the silence with a dry

statement. 'Men like that don't surrender. But they would fly a white flag to make us walk out there to meet them and, with well-placed gunmen, kill every damned one of us. I have seen it happen.' Flaherty looked at the priest. 'If you think it otherwise, walk over there.' Flaherty paused, then sourly said: 'Go ahead, Father. You're a man of God. He'll protect you.'

Among the listeners were people who did not like the way Flaherty had talked to the priest, but nothing was said, and Father Damion did go to the doorway, looking out where dancing heat waves were in place even though it was still early morning.

Efraim Montoya loudly protested. 'Father, the *gringo* is right. They will kill you.'

The priest faced around, smiling. 'There is one of them coming this way with both arms over his head.'

Several villagers crowded the doorway. The first one to turn back was bleakly smiling. 'I've seen that one.'

Father Damion stepped outside and greeted the filthy, haggard, unshaven man and got back a reply in hoarse Spanish. 'There is no water. We will trade you an old injured white-headed man for water.'

Father Damion held one of the spindle doors for the renegade to pass through. The renegade halted, dropped both arms, and seemed surprised to see so many armed women. He repeated what he had said outside and did not move until someone broke the silence that ensued. Fulgencio Aramas, the caféman who rarely spoke, said: 'I know you. You ate at my café. You and another man ... when you first came to San Ildefonso.'

The renegade looked stonily at the massive man. He said: '*Amigo,* your coffee would float lead.' The renegade faced Lázaro Guardia. 'Will you trade or will we begin by breaking the old man's legs, then his arms, and gouge his eyes out.'

That was too much for Isabel Montenegro. She called the renegade names her own husband would have taken an oath she did not know.

The renegade smiled. 'Water, *señora,* and the old man will stay alive.' The man faced Lázaro again, but before he could speak Father Damion said: 'There is a well with a bucket on a pulley.'

The renegade stopped smiling. 'A man who was dying tried to pull up water and fell into the well. We let him sink, then lowered the bucket. It came up pink.'

Juan Bohorquez invited the renegade to share *pulque* with him, but the renegade refused. He faced Lázaro again. 'You are the *jefe.* We have watched you. You are the one who says things others do. We need buckets of water, and the people to carry them.'

Lázaro snorted. 'We'll give you water, all

you can carry. If you need more, get some of your companions to come for more water in buckets.'

The renegade had close-spaced eyes like a snake that seemed rarely to blink as he regarded Guardia. 'I can carry two buckets. We need many more. We have the wounded who cry for water.'

Lázaro nodded at the saloonman. 'Do you have two buckets, Juan?'

'I have four.'

'Fill them and bring them to this ... man.'

Nothing more was said until four full buckets of water had been put on the floor in front of the venomous-eyed renegade. He looked steadily at Lázaro, ignoring the buckets. 'The stout woman who curses so well can carry two. I will carry two.'

Isabel walked slowly across the room, stopped in front of the renegade, and flashed her right hand. When the knife point pricked the man's middle, he instinctively sucked back. Isabel said: 'Take up all four *merda de los Satanás*,' and pushed a little harder with the knife.

The renegade did not move. His unblinking stare at José Montenegro's wife was like wet obsidian. He shook his head.

Fulgencio Aramas walked over, lifted two buckets in one hand and repeated it with the other two buckets. He held them for the renegade to take. The man showed discolored teeth in a wolfish smile and shook his head again. The caféman put the buckets down, grabbed the renegade's shirt, lifted the man a foot off the floor, and then let him fall.

The renegade rolled over and sprang back upright. This time he had a knife, and it was shiny, sharp, and long with a slight up-curving tip.

Fulgencio Aramas stood like a rock.

The renegade hesitated, then sheathed the knife, and forced another smile. 'If I don't get back...'

Fulgencio Aramas spoke again. 'If you don't get back, there will be one less. I'm going to break your neck.'

As if by magic the knife appeared. The caféman leaned away and then, moving with speed rare in a man of his heft, caught the knife arm, brought it down hard over a bent knee, and everyone in the room heard the man try to stifle a scream. Fulgencio picked up the knife while the renegade was bent over, holding his sprained arm with the other hand. The caféman picked up one bucket at a time and hurled the contents at the renegade.

The man's teeth were locked as he raised his face slightly. 'I'm goin' to roast you like a pig,' he snarled.

Fulgencio Aramas slowly raised a mighty right arm and fired a rock-hard fist. The renegade went down in a heap with one arm twisted unnaturally beneath him.

Efraim Montoya jumped up and down. 'Now what do we do? He could have had the water. We could have traded for Tomás Henriques. Now...?'

The caféman lifted Efraim Montoya with one hand and threw him against the bar. Except for the *curandero's* lamentations and groans, the saloon was deathly silent.

Eventually Torres Mendoza softly said: 'That is that. They get no water. There is now one less of them ... and what about us?'

He got no answer.

It required time, but eventually the soaked and battered renegade rolled over, spat blood, and, using one arm, got unsteadily to his feet. Lázaro was waiting. He jerked his head and pushed a bench in place for the renegade. The man favoured his injured arm. Lázaro got *pulque* from Juan Bohorquez, watched the renegade swallow, took back the bottle, and fished something from his pocket. It was the map Father Damion had showed him earlier.

The renegade's eyes cleared. New color came into his face. He looked around for the caféman, studied him until Lázaro tapped the man's chest, spread out the soiled little map, and pointed. 'That is mission San Luis Rey.' The renegade wiped blood from his swelling mouth and blew out a ragged breath as Lázaro pointed. 'Look, you! That is Albu-querque. That line is the Pecos River. Down here more than a hundred miles is San Ildefonso. Are you listening? Do you see those words?'

The renegade held a soiled bandanna to his mouth as he looked at the scrap of cloth. For seconds he held the bandanna to his mouth without moving. He slowly bent closer, using a finger from his uninjured arm to trace marks on the map. When he raised his eyes, Lázaro said: 'It is there? Do you comprehend? The Spanish treasure is at Mission San Luis Rey. A man who died ... named Otero ... had this map. You haven't seen it before?'

The renegade barely shook his head, still holding the bandanna to his swelling lower face. There was pain, but for a moment he alternately looked at Lázaro Guardia and the map. He spoke, and, although the words were difficult to understand in the deathly quiet room, what he said was comprehensible. 'We knew Pedro Otero and his brother. Pedro Otero told us the treasure was here.'

Lázaro shrugged. 'Why would he do that? So that you would come here, and maybe so that he could go to San Luis Rey and not have to share?' Lázaro shrugged again. 'I don't know. Pedro Otero is dead. So is his brother, Joáquin.'

The renegade lowered the bandanna, inspected the blood, and held it to his lower face again. He got unsteadily to his feet, crossed the silent room to the doors, and pushed on through. Someone said: 'The water!'

The renegade did not return. Several villagers came to look at the map. They had known nothing of the map, and most of them had not believed there was hidden treasure. Not in any of the old missions. Now, having heard the exchange between *el jefe* and the renegade, the legend they had grown up with clearly was uppermost in their minds.

Several stubborn people, including Rafael Cardinál and Juan Bohorquez, leaned over the map, scowling. A woman quietly said – 'I never believed! – and no one looked at her.

The villagers remained silent for a long time. A belief they had matured with had in moments been questioned. Something like that required time to become accustomed to.

Several men left the saloon to scout. When one of them returned, he reported to their leader: 'There is a light up there, and something is going on.'

Lázaro joined others to go as far north as the last few buildings. The freighter, accompanied by William carrying a rifle, stood slightly apart. The freighter said: 'They got horses,' and added to that: 'Water! That son-of-a-bitch didn't want water. He wanted to look for horses.'

It was difficult to see well, except for the occasional squeal of a horse. It was difficult to make out figures even when they were moving.

Flaherty spoke. 'They're leaving, what's left of them. Lázaro, is that map gen-u-ine? If it is...'

Someone yonder called out sharply in Spanish. 'No. No! We don't have that many horses.'

The villagers were quiet enough so that, when the riders left the mission, heading north, they could hear them. Efraim Montoya said: 'They left the ones unable to ride. We have enough hurt people at the *cantina*.'

Juan Bohorquez tapped the priest's shoulder and jerked his head. No one tried to stop them. Instead, they remained still and motionless watching the saloonman and the holy man walk in the direction of the mission.

It was growing dark and was still. For once there was a slight ground swell of a breeze. An older man came up behind the watchers. Moses Morisco spoke very quietly. *'¿Amigos, qué paso?'*

Agitated, Efraim Montoya answered. No one else even looked around. 'They got horses and have ridden away northward.'

Moses Morisco found a rock and sat down. When candles were lighted in the church and brightened the evening, the storekeeper spoke softly again. 'Defiling a temple brings God's wrath.'

As before no one heeded the older man. Part of the reason was that Juan Bohorquez came outside and called that only the dead and dying were left. Of seven injured men five had died. The two still alive had been propped against a wall. When the villagers arrived, they gazed fixedly at them. The only renegade who knew English said: 'Is there really such a map?'

Lázaro nodded and replied in the same language. 'It is true. The Otero brothers knew about it. They deliberately led you to the wrong place.'

'Where are they?'

'They're dead.'

The speaker looked at the man propped beside him and spoke again. 'And so is he. Don't move him. He is bleeding inside.'

Patrick Flaherty, a practical man, looked at the sprawled corpses and shook his head. He had seen cannons fired many times. What he hadn't seen up close was the result. He addressed the priest. 'They've got to be buried.'

Father Damion gave Last Rites to the hemorrhaging *guerrillero*. The man seemed not to hear. Within moments he sagged against his companion and toppled forward.

194

Two women arrived, looked almost indifferently at the bodies, and disappeared more deeply into the church. Father Damion followed them. They found Tomás Henriques lying across his rifle. One of the women touched him, and he groaned. She called for help in carrying him to the saloon. His shirt was soaked with blood from the shoulder wound, and he had been beaten. He had moments of lucidity. During one such moment he recognized the men who came to carry him. He feebly smiled and said– 'He takes a long time.' –and lapsed into unconsciousness.

There were stars but no moon. The path to the village was faintly visible for those carrying the injured renegade and Tomás Henriques. A few people lingered at the mission to retrieve weapons and empty the pockets of the dead who would have no use for money, watches, silver inlaid spurs, even several valuable belt buckles of silver and gold.

Bohorquez's *cantina* was again the hospital. Several of the wounded villagers, who were able, helped with the old man and the surviving renegade who was very young and asked for the priest. Father Damion took the man's confession with lowered head. The young renegade had committed atrocities of a nature that sickened the holy man, but his purpose was not to judge – it was to intercede and to offer forgiveness.

Chapter Thirteen

Aftermath

For the first time in days the women put aside their weapons and ransacked the houses and Morisco's store for enough food to make decent meals. When daylight returned, Father Damion recruited gravediggers and others who would fetch the dead renegades. Dead horses were dragged a mile away and left. Those with bridles, blankets, and saddles were stripped. José Montenegro sweated with the others without speaking even when his wife spoke to him.

Tomás Henriques was given food and ate like a horse. The women salved his bruises and bandaged places where he bled, including the gash where a bullet had grazed his shoulder. He slept. So did others who were not dragooned by the holy man. There had been little time for sleep for several days.

It was evening when Father Damion went to the graves of villagers killed during the fight. Maria Alvarez was buried with the others. Lázaro and Rafael Cardinál were in attendance. Rafael said: 'When I was younger, I knew her. She wasn't crazy then.

Tomás Alvarez, her son, and I played together. She made the best *entomotados* I ever ate.'

Lázaro had known the old woman, but as a youngster he had been afraid of her. He asked about her husband, and, although his companion and he knew the old woman and her son well, neither had ever seen Tomás Alvarez's father. All Rafael remembered was that Maria Alvarez's husband went to Mexico and never returned. 'Dead for a fact,' Rafael Cardinál said. 'Stories came back that he had been a leader of *guerrilleros*.'

What troubled the women as much as the dead was the condition of their homes when they returned to them. In one house, which was thick with blue-tailed flies, they called for men to haul away an old grandfather whose throat had been slashed from ear to ear. After this was done, one woman sat a long time in shade behind the house. It would take more than soap and water. The entire inside of the *jacal* would have to be whitewashed. The family to which the old dead grandfather belonged was never able to explain how and why the old man had been in the house where he had been killed. He was not even distantly related to those who lived in that house.

There would be more questions without answers, nor could all the dead be buried in one day. The ground was like iron for almost two feet down. After that there was moisture which made digging easier, but there was too much digging for it all to be accomplished in one day quickly.

Patrick Flaherty and William walked out to the goat ranch where penned animals had been without water for several days. They hauled water until they had to sit on the porch of the house. Patrick Flaherty knew nothing about goats except that they smelled. William had names for some of the goats and got Flaherty to go with him when he turned the goats out to forage.

While the goats grazed, Flaherty and William found shade and made desultory conversation. The boy asked about freighting, a subject about which Pat Flaherty conversed easily. When he lapsed into silence, the boy said: 'We could sell the goats and buy you another wagon.'

Flaherty smiled. 'It takes three spans of mules or horses to pull freight wagons.'

William was undaunted. 'We can round up some of the loose horses.'

'Them's saddle animals, son. Draft critters is bigger and heavier.'

William remained undaunted. 'We can get them. Where there's a will, there's a way.'

Flaherty gazed at the boy in long silence. William hadn't heard that saying from Mexicans. He'd probably heard it from his father. Flaherty leaned back in shade and fell asleep.

For two days the people of San Ildefonso worked long hours removing what remained of Isabel Montenegro's barricade at the lower end of the village. Although it appeared the fight was over, people who had known each other all their lives and were generally intermarried did not recover quickly from burying the dead. Mostly, after setting their little houses to rights and cooking large communal meals, the women went to the mission cemetery with rosaries dangling from callused hands, and each in her own way shed tears as she prayed. It was for most villagers the worst interlude of their lives. As long as they lived, they would cherish the day of the dead.

The last person to be buried was José Montenegro. He was found beside the little brass cannon. Why he had died, no one knew, although the *curandero,* an individual who had an explanation for all illnesses and deaths, told Isabel Montenegro her husband's heart had stopped, and, of course, the old skinny scarecrow was right, because whatever else might cause death, it could not occur until the heart stopped.

Francesca Cardinál and other women could spend more time with the wounded, most of whom, since being injured days earlier, were recovering, despite having been cared for only intermittently during the fighting. Moses Morisco told Juan Bohorquez that, despite what the priest said, people did not die until it was ordained that they should, and Juan set up a bottle of local wine. He and the storekeeper drank together. As Moses Morisco was turning to go, he told Juan Bohorquez it was time for him to leave the village, and the saloonman was too stunned at the announcement to ask why. The reason was elementary. Moses Morisco had used up his inventory, food, ammunition, cloth for bandages, even his hoard of dynamite. He had bankrupted himself, and, regardless that people thought he had a miser's wealth hidden away, Morisco had never operated on other than a cash-and-carry basis with his suppliers. Now he had no cash with which to restock his store. Later, when Juan Bohorquez sat next to him at Fulgencio Aramas's eatery, the storekeeper said: 'I came here twenty years ago because it was said the railroad would arrive in a few years. It never arrived, did it?'

'Where will you go?' Bohorquez asked.

'I have relatives in New York City.'

Juan slumped against the counter. 'We will miss you. Without you San Ildefonso won't even have a store.'

'It didn't have a store when I came here. Tell me, Juan ... I will need a horse and a wagon.'

'I'll find them for you,' Bohorquez said,

rising to put several coins beside his empty platter. He spoke in Spanish. 'May God always be with you.'

Morisco looked up and said: 'Juan, in my lifetime, I've survived hardships without His help. Tell me, old friend, where was He when those murderers attacked the village?'

The news spread that Moses Morisco was leaving. It added to the troubled mood of the villagers. For Lázaro Guardia this additional blow was augmented when he went to his corral yard and found that six horses were missing. He would send a report of this and the reason for it to the stage company's offices in Santa Fé and had no doubt about the response. Forthright Stage & Freight Company would end all runs south to San Ildefonso.

As the two-day aftermath wore along, discouragement increased. Father Damion brought women to his mission to help clean the place. It was a filthy shambles. Bottles of sacramental wine that hadn't been emptied had been hurled against the walls. Even scrubbing and whitewash would not disguise the smell. Fortunately it was not a wholly unpleasant aroma since it would linger for a long time.

When evening arrived two days after the battle, the priest went out back where so many fresh mounds had been carefully shaped. As yet there were no markers. That would be taken care of in time. Tomás Henriques was sitting on a large stone with hands clasped between his knees. He showed purple bruises, and his soiled, torn shirt was darkly stained where blood had run after he had been grazed over the shoulder. He did not raise his eyes when the priest appeared. The fresh mound a few feet in front of the stone where Henriques sat had a hastily erected marker with a cross and words crudely carved into the wood.

Father Damion sat on another nearby rock. After a long silence he said: 'It was time, Tomás.'

'Yes,' the old man said. 'She was beautiful when we were young, Father.'

The priest nodded. 'What happened, old friend, was God's will.'

Tomás Henriques slowly straightened on his rock. 'You know better, Father. It was my will when I left her with the baby coming and returned fifteen years later. God had nothing to do with it. She didn't know me. She had taken back her maiden name years earlier. When I told her ... when I talked to her ... she went into a crazy rage and threw things at me. She called me a creature of the devil. I went to see her days later. She was kind and even smiled, but she didn't remember my earlier visit. She thought I was a stranger. I did that to her, Father.'

'And you've spent years in atonement in

the mission. Our God is a forgiving God.'

Henriques slumped. '*She* would never forgive me even if she hadn't been *loco en la cabeza*. I did that to her and to her child. She used her own name. When I told her I was her husband, Tomás Henriques, she spat on me, called me a person who lied through his teeth, and came at me like a wild animal. Father, I did that to her. God had nothing to do with it.'

'But you have been forgiven, Tomás. Our Savior is a person of mercy and understanding. You have lived in the church loft many years, and you have asked for absolution every day for all those years. Surely God has cleansed your conscience and your soul.'

The old man's gaze was fixed on the grave of Maria Alvarez. 'You are wrong, Father. If He had cleansed my soul, why, then, do I live night and day in pain for what I did? My conscience is a scourge. If God wills anything, it has to be that He wills me to have haunting dreams and to rise each morning in pain.'

The priest changed the subject. 'I know you have seen young Tomás whom she named after you?'

'*Si*, many times,' Henriques said and considered the clasped hands between his knees. 'A handsome man. Maria brought him up very well.'

Father Damion said nothing. He knew the entire village had brought up Tomás Alvarez after his father had abandoned Maria and their son to go to Mexico. In fact, if that hadn't been the case, Tomás Alvarez and his mother would have starved.

The old man straightened up, gazing at the priest. 'He is one of the best wild horse hunters.'

Father Damion agreed. It had been the old man's son who had helped San Ildefonso with money he got for wild horses he caught. He and the old man had the same build, lean and tall. The old man had spied on young Tomás Alvarez many times, seeking a resemblance. Others had done the same thing. In some ways the wild horse hunter favoured the father he had never known and who, according to local gossip, had been killed in Mexico many years earlier.

A pair of elderly women appeared, both wearing the black *rebozo* of mourning. Tomás Henriques watched them, going among the fresh graves, and jerked his head for the priest to go. Father Damion did. As he approached, both the women covered their faces and cried. Tomás Henriques heard and rose to disappear inside the mission.

The morning of the third day it rained. What baffled the people was that there had not been a cloud in the sky the night before. When it rained on the south desert, it poured. For as long as was possible the ground absorbed water, but there was a limit even in bone-dry desert country. By nightfall with no lessening of the downpour, people stoked up fires and remained indoors. San Ildefonso's one roadway became a river of roiled dun-brown water. In order to prevent water from coming indoors, people build barricades. It was not possible to see from the village to the mission. If it had been possible, it would have been noticeable that there were lighted candles in the chapel. Quite a number of them.

Lázaro Guardia was in his small office at the corral yard when Rafael Cardinál arrived, holding a poncho above his head. As he came in out of the rain and put the poncho aside, he said: 'I was at the *cantina*. One of the boys Juan Bohorquez sent to the *yanqui* fort returned. The soldiers are on their way.'

Lázaro leaned back. 'They come when we don't need them.'

Francesca Cardinál's husband sat down while speaking. 'If people see them, it will help in case there are more raiders coming north. The boy told Juan that Sixto Mejia's rebellion is falling to pieces, that soldiers and *Rurales* are combing the country for revolutionaries to kill.'

Lázaro sighed. 'Let us hope they do not come to San Ildefonso.'

After Rafael Cardinál departed, Lázaro rose to go out where company horses were picking at what was left of an earlier feeding. San Ildefonso was quiet. Few people were abroad. The steel shutters were in place at the store. In the west a small banner of dust rose in the distance. Lázaro went where he could see better. Two people, one tall and one short, were driving goats in the direction of the village. Lázaro shook his head. People kept milk goats for which they had small pens. The only place where a herd of goats could be confined was at Lázaro's mud-walled horse corral which, at the present time, had about a dozen horses in it. He didn't wait but caught the corralled horses two at a time and stalled them in the barn. When he had finished, there was only one unoccupied stall. By this time the sound of driven goats could be heard. People left their houses to watch. Lázaro walked without haste until he could signal with raised arms for the goat drovers to drive their animals into his empty corral.

Flaherty waved back as he and his undersized shadow turned their animals. Fortunately domestic goats were easily herded. They filed into the corral without incident. Lázaro closed the gate as the freighter came up and said: 'If Lopez has no kin, I figure the boy should get the goats.'

Lázaro knew of no kin. Although he and

206

Alfredo Lopez had known one another, Lopez had always been a private individual, almost a hermit. Lázaro looked at the youth who returned the look, showing no expression. Lázaro told the freighter: 'Lopez has no kin in San Ildefonso that I know of. I'll ask around.'

Flaherty nodded. 'If there ain't any, me'n the boy figure to sell the goats so we can get a start on puttin' together a freight outfit.'

Lázaro went to the *cantina* where there were only four or five customers. He asked about the kin of Alfredo Lopez, and one old man wagged his head. 'He came here some time back, about eighteen or twenty years. He came alone except for some goats. I knew him well enough. Used to go out yonder and visit. He came out of Mexico after all his kin had been shot during one of those uprisings. All that was left were some goats. He brought them with him.'

Lázaro found the freighter and William at the café and told them what the old man had said. The boy looked quickly at Flaherty. 'You see? Now we can get a start.'

The freighter winked at Lázaro. 'He'll make a decent partner. I like 'em as never give up.'

Efraim Montoya came to the doorway. 'Lázaro, horses. You can hear them. Tomás Henriques is out front of the mission with a bugle.'

207

As Lázaro left the café, one old man was heading for the door when Juan Bohorquez roughly pushed him aside and reached the roadway as the elfin *curandero* and Lázaro Guardia were hiking northward. The bugle sounded, and once more Lázaro Guardia wondered. He had heard stories about old Henriques – that he had led a band of brutal *guerrilleros*, had committed atrocities some of which Lázaro did not believe. The stories he did believe were bad enough for the white-headed old man to have reason to spend years seeking forgiveness.

When Lázaro saw Tomás Henriques, he was holding a battered old bugle and peering northward. The sound of many horses was muted by distance, but rising dust indicated the way they were coming. When the men from the village approached, Tomás Henriques called to them: 'If it is *Federales,* they will change course. I told them with the bugle ... *parar mientes!* Not to approach the village.'

Juan snorted. 'It won't be Mexican soldiers, Tomás. Not coming from the north.'

The old man was squinting in the distant direction of the dust and seemed not to have heard Bohorquez.

It was not possible to drive wild horses. It was not even always possible to keep them bunched. The watchers at the mission saw the herd. It was a large one. Since *mesteños* ran as individuals, it was Lázaro's opinion that the band must once have been larger. Wild horses ran with terror. Many would veer away. Seasoned mustangers let them go. Their objective was to keep as many as possible going in the direction of the horse trap that was located outside the village.

It was really a large band. The *curandero*, jumping up and down with excitement, yelled that there had to be no less than sixty animals. When it was possible to see them and the three mustangers who were riding hard as flankers and wing riders, Lázaro recognized them. The flanker was Tomás Alvarez, riding straight up. The other two riders were youths with families in San Ilde-fonso. As Lázaro watched, Tomás Alvarez stood in his stirrups and signaled with his hat. The wing riders closed in a little, and the *mesteños* crowded close as they swept past the wide wings of the trap. Six or eight missed the wings altogether and raced wildly to bypass the village. There were two gates. One that was slammed behind the horses and one at the opposite end.

Henriques relaxed slightly as he mumbled, 'I was certain it would be soldiers.'

Lázaro and Juan Bohorquez exchanged a look. *Federales* and *Rurales* were feared with good reason among *pronunciados*. They were shot out of hand by Mexico's regulars. The old man had lived with that dread most of his best years. He would use any ruse, including the bugle calls of the regulars, to mislead them. He avoided the others, went inside the mission, and did not reappear.

It was too far to walk to reach the horse trap. The day was blistering hot, so Juan Bohorquez and Lázaro Guardia returned to the village and separated, Lázaro heading for his corral yard, Juan for his *cantina* where men crowded to hear what the sound of all those horses meant. When Bohorquez explained, Pat Flaherty took William and walked all the way out to the trap. He doubted there would be any thousand-pound animals. Freight wagons required at the very least thousand-pound horses or mules to pull them.

Tomás Alvarez was still out there. His two companions had gone to their homes in the village. Alvarez was a lean, tall man, graying at the temples. He was beating off dust with his hat when the freighter approached, and then he stopped dusting as he smiled. 'The band was three times that size,' he said, and shrugged wide shoulders.

Flaherty went to lean on a fir-log stringer – not the top one, which was six feet from the ground, but the second one.

Tomás Alvarez came over. 'There are six with brands.'

Flaherty had already noticed this. Of those six, four were well over a thousand pounds.

He said: 'I'll buy four.'

Tomás Alvarez nodded. 'Tell me which ones.'

Flaherty described them by markings.

The younger man nodded. 'I think they are broke horses. Three dollars a head.'

On the hike back to the village Flaherty said: 'Twelve dollars, William.'

The boy did as he usually did. He ignored the sound of defeat in Flaherty's voice and said: 'The goats might bring that much.'

Flaherty did not respond. The best milk goat in the entire south desert country did not sell for more than from fifty cents to one dollar, and there were not that many goats.

Chapter Fourteen

The Unexpected!

Time was a healer. As one scorching day followed another, something that would never be effectively disguised – bullet scars – was ignored as life resettled into its time-hallowed routine. Clothes hung from ropes. What could be salvaged from Isabel Montenegro's barricade at the lower end of the settlement was removed. What was beyond use or repair was taken out and piled for burning when winter arrived. The overnight deluge had left runnels in the roadway that people filled.

Juan Bohorquez went to Lázaro Guardia for a horse and wagon. A number of riderless animals had been caught and were now penned among the horses. Lázaro had combination animals – horses broken to harness as well to saddle – but they belonged to the stage company. So Juan went among the houses and found a light spring wagon that he bought for six dollars. He spent another two dollars for a light harness but found no horse to pull the wagon.

Flaherty told him about the branded

horses out at the trap. He went out there and asked Tomás Alvarez about the marked animals. All Alvarez knew was that the branded animals had been running with the mustangs. When Juan offered to buy one of the branded animals, Tomás Alvarez pointed out the only two he could sell. The saloonman selected one that was old. Tomás roped the animal and led it out where Juan could examine it. The horse had scars, a flat chin, and sunken places over his eyes. Tomás said, if the horse wasn't broken to drive, breaking it to pull a wagon shouldn't take long because it was old. Juan Bohorquez bought it for one dollar and led it back to the village where Lázaro used his only empty stall for the horse. He salved its freshest injuries, gave it sparingly of his meager store of grain, and told Bohorquez to return the following day. If the horse knew what driving harness was, Lázaro would find out; and, if he didn't know, Lázaro would teach him.

Juan Bohorquez went to the store where Moses Morisco had several bundles and a battered old round-top steamer trunk in the middle of the store. He also had cartons of whatever had been left on the shelves. Juan was satisfied that he had acquired a wagon with a bed large enough to hold what the old storekeeper had piled together.

Back at the saloon Juan mentioned that the storekeeper would be leaving, probably well before sunrise in the morning. There were questions. Juan answered them frankly. He had found a horse, a wagon, and driving harness. He also said it was obligatory that the villagers show their gratitude. He would buy two goats from the freighter and barbecue them – after nightfall when the heat would be less.

Until this announcement there hadn't been much pleasantry. Now there was. It was a tradition in the Southwest. Fiestas were not only well attended but invariably raised spirits, and right now that was what San Ildefonso needed more than anything else.

Father Damion was at the mission. He was the last one to hear about the barbecue. The person who told him was Tomás Henriques who had heard of it from one of Juan Bohorquez's youngsters who had previously ridden to the fort. There had been two boys who were sent. The second lad had never returned and, in fact, was never heard of again.

Father Damion was on a bench under the overhang that ran the full length of the mission's east side where it was cool. After Henriques departed, he went to asleep. What awakened him was something he knew about but did not mention: intuition. When he opened his eyes and saw the bent figure among the graves, he rose, left his shaded, cool place, and went to where the woman, wearing a black lace *rebozo,* was standing with a rosary dangling from her hands. Her eyes were closed as she prayed. She was unaware of the priest's presence until he stepped on rattling pebbles. She looked at him from an expressionless face as she said: 'He was a good man, Father.'

Father Damion did not return the widow's gaze when he replied. Instead he considered the freshly mounded grave. 'Yes he was, *señora.*'

'He drank, Father. It had him in its grip, but José was a good husband and a person who helped others.'

Father Damion inclined his head. He knew all the tales of José Montenegro's aberrations, some recalled as jokes, others derisively. 'There will be a special place for him,' the priest said.

'He believed, Father. On the days when he was able, we would come to services.'

Again the priest nodded. José Montenegro had not been to services or Mass for many months.

Isabel Montenegro spoke again. 'He was good to me. He was my life, Father. No one knew José as I did. We fought the drinking together. He would cry when he gave in. I would cry with him. I think he died quickly without pain.'

Again the priest nodded. It was very possible. He had been found near the cannon as relaxed as a person asleep.

'I will miss him for the rest of my life, Father.'

'So will we all.'

'Could you say a prayer before the altar, Father?'

'Next Sunday, *señora*, when everyone will be present. Tell me ... is there anything else I can do?'

Isabel Montenegro shook her head, unwilling to trust her voice. As Father Damion departed, she continued praying the beads she had been praying when he had interrupted her.

As the priest moved closer to the cool verandah, he saw the *curandero*, walking in the direction of Isabel Montenegro. He moved where the wiry old man could see him, and beckoned. Efraim Montoya continued toward the widow. Father Damion stepped out into sunlight, cupped his hands, and told the *curandero* it was important – he must see him at once.

That worked. Montoya veered abruptly in the direction of the long, shaded verandah, smiling broadly.

'It was to tell her about the fiesta tonight at the *cantina* because Moses Morisco is leaving,' Montoya said, and eased down upon a bench. It was cool. The verandah's dirt runway had been meticulously paved with adobe bricks.

The *curandero* asked what it was the priest had to say, and Father Damion had to rummage his thoughts because he really did not have anything to say. 'Well, *viejo*, you were right about the cause of José Montenegro's passing.'

Montoya's chest swelled. 'I am usually right. No one can cure and heal for as long as I have and not become vastly experienced. Father, what killed José was liquor. I have seen it many times. When the heart can no longer accept the poison, it stops. Is that all, Father?'

'Efraim, please ... leave José's widow at peace. There is nothing you or I can say that will help. *¿Sabe?*'

'*Sí*, I only wanted to tell her of the wonders of the place where José now is.'

'Let me do that, Efraim.'

The *curandero* stood up. 'Of course. There will be a fiesta tonight behind the *cantina* to send Moses Morisco on his way. You will be there?'

'Certainly.' The priest watched Montoya change course, heading for the village, sighed, and rose. He was dusting the altar – doing a small chore that the cleaning women had not overlooked but that required a priest's particular attention – when he heard someone shout. The voice was pitched high and excited. Father Damion went outside. He did not immediately see the boy atop the saloon until he yelled twice more and waved his arms. It was the lad who had returned from going to the fort and had told Tomás Henriques of the fiesta. Father Damion did as others also did. He assumed the watcher on the roof had seen *yanqui* soldiers and returned to the mission where heat rarely reached.

The walls were three-feet thick and prevented noise from being heard. There were also a number of high, slitted windows for sunlight. The real reason for those slitted high windows was to prevent Indian arrows from killing people among the pews, but there had been no Indian attacks in many years.

Juan Bohorquez sent another lad to the mission to tell Father Damion that riders were coming helter-skelter from the south and that even farther south, where it hadn't rained, there was a second banner of dust. The lad told the priest it was the opinion of Juan Bohorquez that the second party of horsemen was chasing the first band. He also said it was the saloonman's guess that the horsemen racing toward San Ildefonso had to be remnants of Sixto Mejia's failed rebellion.

The priest returned to the village with the excited youth. The people were like headless chickens, running every which way. Among the women who ran were those who had left their rifles at home.

Rafael Cardinál and Pat Flaherty were arguing in the center of the road. Rafael gestured wildly with both arms. The freighter had a voice that carried. He was yelling for the villagers to hasten to the south end, get among the last houses, and be ready when the men out of Old Mexico came. Rafael was arguing that the people with weapons should fight from their houses, snipe, and utilize good cover.

Flaherty was red-faced. As the priest arrived, so did Juan Bohorquez. They both took the freighter's side, and Rafael stopped gesturing as he said: 'And if we can't stop them before they enter the village?'

'Then,' Juan Bohorquez said, 'we can fall back and do as you wish. We did it before and won.'

The freighter squinted hard. He saw dust but no horsemen. He took the boy with him and started briskly for the area where Isabel Montenegro's barricade had once been.

Moses Morisco took his laden wagon, and the old horse to pull it, around behind the store and left them there. When he returned to the roadway, Tomás Alvarez, the wild horse hunter, rushed past, wearing a grim expression. He had no rifle, only a belt gun, and he was hurrying in the direction of the mission.

Efraim Montoya was atop the *cantina* roof,

gesturing and yelling words no one understood. Isabel Montenegro went among the women, gathering them for the fight. They joined the men at the south end of the village. Someone sounded a bugle. Lázaro Guardia's first impression was that it was Tomás Henriques again, and, except that the sound was partially muted by distance, it could have been the white-headed man.

People raised a yell when the hard-riding strangers got close enough for them to be discerned, and, for a fact, some of them wore heavy cartridge belts crossed over their chest. They cry went up: *'¡Bandoleros!'*

North of the village, within walking distance of the mission, men were straining and struggling in the middle of the road to move the little cannon toward the upper end of San Ildefonso. They could move the cannon, but there were not enough to keep it moving, nor had it been loaded.

Torres Mendoza, a dead shot, knelt behind a massive low adobe wall, rested his rifle atop it, and, after careful aim, fired. Those around him thought he had missed, or that the distance was too great. They were wrong. A very dark *bandolero* rode ahead about fifty feet before slowly leaning far to one side and falling from his horse. The animal veered wildly to the west and ran for all it was worth.

There was a furious fusillade from the oncoming horsemen. No one was hit, although two scraped rawhide windows were punctured. The *bandoleros* had booted Winchesters, but they returned the fire of Torres Mendoza with pistols. It was no miracle that the defenders were not injured. Hand guns had limited range. Firing them from the saddles of racing horses made a hit accidental. The *bandoleros* were riding for their lives. There was no time to consider the reason that they were heading directly for the village. If there had been, two explanations would have sufficed: they wanted cover among the *jacales,* and their horses had been ridden too hard and were beginning to stumble.

Isabel Montenegro, the iron will of defiance showing in her face, did not raise an arm and lower it for the women until Lázaro yelled. The ensuing gunsmoke clouded the vision of both attackers and defenders until several riderless horses raced past up the roadway, stirrups flapping.

The fusillade of the women caused the second rank of *bandoleros* to yell and gesture for those behind them to follow, as they reined to the west. Not all made it. Gunfire from the defenders was deafeningly incessant. More riderless animals raced up the roadway.

Not all the *bandoleros* saw the signal to go around the village or, having seen it, kept their straight-on approach, firing. Defenders turned to rake the riders in the roadway. If

221

any were hit, there was no sign of it. But something else happened that broke and scattered them, those fortunate enough to get clear. A solid wall of wild horses entered the village from the north. They filled the roadway from side to side and ran in wild-eyed terror.

The *bandoleros* screamed and fought to rein among the houses. The wild horses charged into and over the mounted raiders. The villagers watched now in stunned silence without firing a shot. None of them, not even the oldest among them, had ever seen such a sight. Wild horses trampled down raiders, knocking the horses of *bandoleros* off their feet. There were gunshots among the desperate riders, and mustangs fell, but there were too many. The others, terrorized by the noise, the gunshots, the screams and yells, made no effort to avoid collisions. Far back Tomás Alvarez stood in the roadway with a carbine that he did not raise.

Lázaro Guardia encountered the priest, with a carbine, and paused to wipe off sweat, then left Father Damion to hasten northward where he met Tomás Alvarez and yelled to him over the noise. 'You saved the village.'

Alvarez called back. 'Look, there is a larger band approaching.'

That bugle that had been heard earlier sounded again, and this time it was closer. Lázaro stepped aside and saw Tomás Henriques, standing outside the church, looking northward with one shading hand above his eyes. The old man had no bugle.

The wild horses raced southward, cleared the last buildings, and began to flee in different directions, still racing belly-down.

For a long moment there was no gunfire, then it began, systematic and at spaced intervals. Alvarez called again to Lázaro Guardia: *'¡Los perdigones!'*

Lázaro did not reply. If *bandoleros* were placed against a wall and shot, it could not be very many. The wild horses had ground many others to mincemeat.

Tomás Henriques came southward from the mission, seeking Father Damion. He did not find him, which may have been just as well. A holy man, using a saddle gun, might have shaken the old man's faith, if not in his Maker, then possibly in priests.

The sun was high with that faded color of old copper that went with intense heat. There was very little work done, dragging carcasses from the roadway. Juan Bohorquez, sweating like a stud horse, told Lázaro one woman had been injured by a flying block of adobe, and Rafael Cardinál had a wrenched ankle, acquired when he looked over his shoulder and saw that solid wall of wild-eyed mustangs, racing toward the center of town. Juan said: 'Rafael could never run, even when we were children.'

Efraim Montoya climbed back onto the *cantina's* roof. For a while he squinted without yelling, but, when the *cantina* was full of grimy defenders needing water, too tired to do more than slump in silence, the *curandero* began yelling and jumping up and down again. Before anyone left the saloon, the massive caféman, Fulgencio Aramas, made one of his extremely rare pronouncements. 'I think I will climb up there and strangle that poultice-maker of dead chickens.' But Aramas did not move from his chair, and for a long time neither did anyone else. Meantime the old prune atop the roof yelled and howled and cursed.

Lázaro looked at the exhausted defenders of both sexes. 'It will be the others, coming from the south. Let's take places at the lower end of the village again.' He did not ask how the ammunition was holding out, which was just as well. Some of the men had half a pocketful, but among the *amazonas* there were fewer than ten rounds, and then only if they shared what they had.

As Lázaro went to the doorway where dancing waves of heat shimmered in the roadway, Tomás Henriques was entering. He yielded the right of way, and, as Lázaro stepped outside, Tomás spoke in Spanish. 'Soldiers of the bloody gridiron.' He pointed northward.

Lázaro slitted his eyes. The soldiers were aligned in two extended ranks. There were two blue uniforms slightly to the west and out front. One held aloft a little swallow-tailed guidon with numbers on it. The second man held aloft the American flag. Lázaro spoke over his shoulder to the defenders inside where it was cool. They crowded outside, even Rafael Cardinál, assisted by his wife.

The blue lines were west of the village and moving at a steady walk. As the watchers shaded their eyes, a rag-headed Indian came from the south and conferred with two officers as the line of march continued. Unsmiling Genero Salas raised an arm pointing southward where a large contingent of Mexican cavalrymen with *Rurales* among them had come to a dead halt, something their ridden-down horses would have appreciated more if there had been shade and water.

The *curandero* called down from the roof. 'There is going to be a big fight. Those Mexicans are in uniform, invading our country.'

The only person to look up was the freighter who said: 'If it's our country, how come you're as dark as dirt, an' I ain't?'

Montoya's head disappeared. The others could have been deaf. Four soldiers in blue left their ranks, the others halting in place, and rode slowly toward the Mexicans. Three Mexican soldiers left their command and rode just as slowly to meet the men in blue, one of whom was a flag bearer, but the Mexicans either had no flag or chose not to show it.

Throughout San Ildefonso the silence was deafening. Tomás Henriques moved among the watchers to stand to the right and slightly behind Tomás Alvarez. He did not speak. The priest had left his saddle gun in the saloon. He tried to make a count of both parties of soldiers and failed. Heat waves made such a count impossible.

Where the two parties came together, there was a brief moment of confusion. The American officer did not speak Spanish, and the heavy-set Mexican officer did not speak English. They resolved this by calling forth an American soldier from the ranks. The American officer dismounted. The heavy-set Mexican remained in the saddle. Whatever was said seemed to have less to do about Mexicans invading New Mexico, an American territory, then it had to do with the heat. Both officers sent riders back to their ranks, and, before the soldiers of both nations began moving toward San Ildefonso from opposite directions, the commanding officers rode at a walk toward the village, conversing through the interpreter.

Juan Bohorquez said: 'They will want water.' He disappeared inside his saloon.

Lázaro asked Fulgencio Aramas to come

with him to the corral yard to help draw water for the horses. The massive caféman went southward with Lázaro without a word, but, when they reached the corral yard, he said: 'If one touches a gun, I will break all their necks.'

Chapter Fifteen

A Dying Village

The heavy-set Mexican officer was dark and so soaked with sweat that his tunic was soggy and rumpled. He was a general. His face bore pock marks, and he talked so fast the interpreter had difficulty keeping up. The North American officer was either a good listener or had something else in mind because, as the small cavalcade entered the village, the *yanqui* studied the silent and still villagers. Lázaro recognized him as did others. He had been in San Ildefonso only a few weeks earlier. He was Captain Frank Bonham, and, as he dismounted in front of the *cantina*, he smiled at Isabel Montenegro who did not smile back.

While the two officers entered the saloon where it was cool and shady, their separate commands remained apart, the full length of the village separating them. Lázaro and Fulgencio Aramas asked the Mexicans to help them water the horses. The *Federales* volunteered quickly until there were more soldiers than buckets.

Lázaro left the caféman to supervise and

228

went up to the saloon where Juan Bohorquez was pouring *pulque* as fast as the Mexican drank it. Captain Bonham addressed the interpreter, an Army corporal. 'Tell General Tapia, he and his command are my prisoners. Ask him if he didn't know he was in United States territory when he chased those *bandoleros*.'

General Tapia was an affable man, either by nature or necessity. He was not only outnumbered, he had violated the treaty of boundaries of two nations. He drank *pulque* and told the interpreter he was unaware that he had crossed into *Los Estados Unidos*, to which Captain Bonham put a disbelieving look at the Mexican, ignored the glass of *pulque* Juan Bohorquez had poured for him, and again addressed the interpreter.

'Tell him there are cairns of whitewashed stones every mile.'

General Tapia made an exaggerated gesture with wide-flung arms. He had seen no such stones.

A soldier came to the saloon to whisper to Captain Bonham, who spoke in English to the soldier. 'Tell him to take them, and the rig, if he can swear he owns them.'

General Tapia mopped sweat and unctuously smiled. He knew no English but thought two of the words sounded like the words in Spanish that meant 'to the wall'.

He toasted Captain Bonham, got a refill,

and toasted *Los Estados Unidos*. As he emptied the second glass, he spoke hurriedly to the interpreter, who addressed the captain. 'He says he'll have his men stack their weapons in the roadway, all of them, which will make it murder if the *nortamericanos* start shooting.'

Bonham was puzzled until he and the interpreter talked, then the captain nodded at General Tapia. 'Tell him to give the order, all weapons are to be stacked as he offered. Tell him their support wagon with its mules will remain here. Tell him that after his animals have been cared for and rested, he can take his command and go back to Mexico, but if any turn back...' Captain Bonham ran a rigid finger across his own throat.

It required time for the interpreter to do his job, but, as he spoke in Spanish, the general's apprehensive expression diminished. When the interpreter finished, the general told Juan Bohorquez to refill the glasses, and this time the general held his small glass out until Captain Bonham brushed it with his glass, and both men drank.

When General Tapia would have left the *cantina* with his escort, Captain Bonham shook his head. 'Tell him he stays until the guns have been stacked, the wagon and mules have been taken away, and his command starts south. Tell him, if my orders aren't carried out to the letter, I will shoot the son-of-a-bitch.'

The interpreter had no difficulty until he came to the part of the general's mother having been a dog. There was no way in Spanish to make an exact interpretation, so the soldier improvised. 'The last thing he said to you, General, is that he will personally cut off your *cajones* if his orders aren't obeyed.'

General Tapia's eyes widened, but he said nothing. Instead, he nodded his head.

The day was wearing along. As the weapons were piled up, San Ildefonso's inhabitants watched in stone-faced silence, and the *Federales* were equally as silent as well as sullen.

Lázaro, who had listened to the exchange between the American captain and the Mexican general, left the saloon to join the villagers. Subordinate officers of the Mexican command supervised the withdrawal southward. General Tapia, soaked with sweat and not entirely steady, offered his hand to Frank Bonham, who shook it and jerked his head. The general and his small entourage went to the center of the roadway and walked southward where soldiers were waiting with horses.

At the north end of the village, soldiers in blue uniforms, carrying carbines, remained in place until the withdrawing invaders were distant enough to seem to be moving about a foot off the ground because of the heat waves. Bonham turned, saw Lázaro, and asked if what he had been told was the truth. Lázaro said it was. The support wagon, that had trailed some distance behind the *Federales* and its animals, was the same outfit that had been stolen from Pat Flaherty. He also told the officer the wagon had a supply of food.

With dusk approaching, Captain Bonham sent a sergeant to tell the soldiers to go to the corral yard and make a meal out of what was in the freight wagon while he, Lázaro Guardia, and several others went to the café where the sweat-drenched, unsmiling, massive caféman fed them without saying a word. Lázaro mentioned the captain's earlier visit and the consequences of it for San Ildefonso. Frank Bonham gazed at Lázaro with eyes that ironically twinkled and went on eating, without saying a word.

There was no barbecue for Moses Morisco because, during the time after the Mexicans had withdrawn and Lázaro had supper with Captain Bonham at the café, Moses Morisco had taken advantage of failing daylight to leave San Ildefonso with the old horse pulling his heavily laden wagon.

Captain Bonham and his soldiers camped at the lower end of the village. The last bugle call the villagers heard was an hour or two before sunrise when the soldiers were roused for departure. A number of people went as far as the lower end of San Ildefonso to watch, and by the time the sun was up and climbing, once again the villagers pitched in to drag dead horses far out and leave them, and to organize burial details.

Father Damion was at the cemetery whose recent inhabitants had swelled it beyond anyone's expectations. One of Isabel Montenegro's *amazonas* asked the priest if he would baptize the Indian woman's grandchild. Father Damion said that, of course, he would, but at the present time he was too occupied. Genero Salas was leaning on a shovel nearby and wondered aloud how it was that Father Damion could be too busy when God never was. The priest eventually went with the woman to perform the baptism, and Genero Salas went back to digging.

The only other person who had heard the exchange at close range smiled, something he hadn't done in a long time. It probably made it easier for him to smile because old Henriques was digging on one side of a grave and Tomás Alvarez was digging opposite him. They talked about recent events. Maria's son said he thought he would leave San Ildefonso because it did not seem to him that it had a future beyond the day-to-day existence that had been its routine for a hundred years.

Henriques paused at his digging. 'But your mother is buried here.'

'I can come back to visit,' the mustanger replied. 'She was never happy here.'

Henriques answered quickly. '*Sí*, she was.'

Tomás Alvarez paused at his digging to lean on the shovel. 'When? Not that I can remember.'

The white-headed man resumed digging without looking up. 'When she was young.'

Tomás Alvarez replied bluntly. 'Before we were abandoned,' he said, and went back to digging.

Henriques did not speak again until the grave was deep enough, and then he disappeared inside the mission.

As before, it required time to recreate order, to give people time to start over again, and this time there was unrest. Juan Bohorquez told Lázaro Guardia he had heard people talking of leaving, of going up to Albuquerque or to Santa Fé, maybe even farther north to Colorado where it was said there were rivers, vast forests, miles of grassland, and work for those still young enough to want to work.

The priest also heard this talk, and it bothered him because maintaining the old mission and a priest in attendance had been a burden. The Mother Church had limits to its magnanimity and compassion – economic limits. If the old mission at San Ildefonso lost

234

even a small part of its congregation, it was possible that the Mother Church would do as had been done throughout the Southwest: hold one final service, then reassign the priest, and abandon the mission. There were dozens of missions founded by Spaniards whose only inhabitants were now birds.

To Father Damion, who was not a young man, San Ildefonso was more than his charge, his parish – it was his family. There was not a person he did not know as well as he might have known his own family, if he'd had one. It was his custom, and had been for years, to sit out on the eastern verandah with a glass of wine and consider the graves whose inhabitants he had for the most part known very well. He would sit there in the dusk with his wine, smiling in remembrance.

It was several weeks after the soldiers of two nations had departed that Pat Flaherty came by with William whom the villagers now had begun calling the freighter's shadow. Flaherty told Father Damion that his animals had been fed, and he would now go north and resume freighting, and that he would take William with him.

Father Damion wished Flaherty well. After all, it wasn't as though a native would be leaving. Freighters by the nature of their occupation did not remain long in any one place. The priest asked when Flaherty intended to leave and was told there was some work to be done to the under-carriage of his wagon, that the Mexicans had bent one axle and had warped a wheel, things it would require time to rectify.

'In a few days,' Flaherty said.

Father Damion told Flaherty they would visit again before the freighter left and winked at William as the two left.

Tomás Henriques came out to enjoy the dusk and mentioned the son only Henriques and the priest knew about. When Father Damion mentioned the probability of the mission being abandoned, Henriques reacted as though he had been stung.

'Why would the Church do that?'

'The parish doesn't pay its way, Tomás, and if people leave San Ildefonso...?' The priest shrugged.

Old Tomás went inside, and Father Damion walked pensively back to the village where Lázaro Guardia met him outside the store, still with its steel shutters in place. Before the priest could mention his problem, Lázaro took him to the cantina where it was cool and where Juan Bohorquez nodded to them as he poured and set thick mugs of *cerveza* before two old men, his only other patrons for the time being.

Father Damion brooded. Lázaro noticed it and made an inquiry that brought the priest's trouble out in a flood of words. Lázaro knew people were going to leave, but it hadn't occurred to him what this would mean to the only church for many miles. There was a house of worship up in Chinle, but the Indians who had built it worshipped in their own way. Lázaro nodded in the direction of the bar, and Juan Bohorquez brought two glasses of wine. Over time a saloonman learned the choices of his patrons. Priests never – almost never – drank anything but wine.

Father Damion saluted Lázaro before sipping. When he put his glass down, he said: 'Old Tomás will continue to live in the bell tower.'

Lázaro nodded. 'From the stories I've heard, he needs all the absolution he can get, Father.'

Whatever the holy man might have said was left unsaid when Tomás Henriques came in, went to the bar, brought his small glass of *aguardiente* to the table, sat down, and considered the priest, ignoring Lázaro. 'If no one left,' he said to the holy man, 'if there was reason for them to stay...?'

Father Damion said: 'What could keep them from leaving?' He gestured with both arms. 'What is there to keep them here. Why would anyone want to stay with *guerrilleros*, running wild from south of the border?'

Lázaro reached indifferently into a pocket, brought forth a very old and soiled scrap of cloth, and, with his companions watching, spread the cloth out and smoothed it with both hands. He then addressed the white-headed man. 'The story of Spanish gold being at our mission is incorrect. Look, you, that is San Luis Rey, that is Albuquerque, and that is the Pecos River. Here we are away down here. Do you comprehend, old friend? The Spanish treasure is up at San Luis Rey.'

Tomás Henriques face, already deeply lined, wrinkled even more as he forgot his liquor to lean and study the old map. The priest, who had already seen the map, and Lázaro Guardia exchanged knowing looks. Henriques took his time, examining the map before straightening back, as he said: *'Gentes de razón,* it is a very old map. Father, tell me honestly what you believe.'

The priest was candid. 'I think the treasure is at San Luis Rey. The Otero brothers knew that but brought *guerrilleros* to attack San Ildefonso as a distraction while they went up to San Luis Rey.'

The priest faintly smiled, but Lázaro, to whom this was something new, stared at Tomás Henriques in silence before he said: 'They didn't want to share with the *guerrilleros.'*

Henriques agreed. 'Why would they? They didn't have to show them the map.' He gulped his drink. 'The promise of riches would be all it would take.'

The priest leaned forward, looking at Lázaro. 'We'll never know where that map came from or how the Oteros found it, but the Oteros believed it. They planned very well. The attack on San Ildefonso was what they wanted so that, while the fighting was going on down here, they could go up to San Luis Rey and plunder the mission.'

Henriques went to the bar for a refill and returned with it. As he sat down, he pushed the map away before speaking. 'All the map does is make for confusion. I think the Oteros knew this. Well, *compañeros,* the Oteros may smile in their graves, thinking they succeeded, but the cache is not at San Luis Rey.'

Lázaro and the priest showed no expression as they stared at Henriques, who was savoring his drink this time and did not speak again until he put the glass down empty.

Father Damion softly said: 'It is here?'

Henriques leaned back from the table, looking at the priest as he said: 'Yes, Father. It is here.' He blew out a flammable breath, ignoring the looks he was getting from the priest and *el jefe.'*

Several villagers entered, saw the conferring men at the table, ignored them to lean against the bar, and ask for beer, which Juan Bohorquez provided as he leaned, jerked his head sideways, and softly said: 'They have some kind of old cloth with drawing on it.'

A beer-drinker looked in the direction of the three seated men, wagged his head, and just as softly said: 'Gustavo and I now own eleven horses, some with saddles. We talked ... there is no one in San Ildefonso with enough money to buy our horses, so we will take them north, get a good price, and keep on riding. San Ildefonso is not just dying, Juan, it is dead.' The speaker made a bleak smile. 'Who will you serve, Juan? No one wants to stay. Too many old ones stayed when they shouldn't have. They are under the ground at the church.'

When the priest came to the bar for three glasses of wine, the owners of the eleven horses brushed the brims of their hats and mumbled something respectful that the priest seemed not to hear as he returned to the table with three full glasses.

Tomás Henriques declined. Ordinarily he drank church wine but never on top of anything stronger.

Lázaro sipped wine as he regarded Tomás. 'Tell me, old friend. Is the treasure at the mission?'

While his companions at the table held their breaths, awaiting a reply, Henriques resettled himself on the chair, gazed dispassionately at Lázaro Guardia's old map, and smiled. He eventually said: 'It is hot out.'

Neither the priest nor *el jefe* commented.

Henriques gazed steadily at the priest.

'How many years have you been at the mission?'

Father Damion answered without hesitation. 'Twelve.'

'And in that time, Father, you went to all places and got to know the missions?'

'Yes, I think so. Tomás...!'

The old man pushed back his chair to rise as he said: 'If you don't mind it being so hot outside and will come with me, I can show you something.'

As Lázaro and the holy man left the saloon with Tomás Henriques, the horse owners at the bar watched the departure and one said: 'I was baptized at the mission. I was pulled by the ear every Sunday when it wasn't raining, to go up there and kneel until my legs ached. Juan, do you believe what the priest says ... that God protects us and is good?'

Bohorquez looked steadily at the speaker. 'This is a poor country for horses, isn't it?'

'Yes. What does that have to do...?'

'And there have never been many horses here, have there? But, now, you and Elfego have eleven horses worth a small fortune. How could that come about in a horseless country? Only through a miracle, Gustavo. Now, tell me, where do miracles originate?'

The swarthy man named Gustavo told his companion to finish his beer and left the saloon to wait outside.

Chapter Sixteen

The Bell Tower

Father Damion walked with an expression of doubt – uneasy doubt, but still doubt. Tomás Henriques paused on the eastern *ramada* to gave in the direction of the graves, new ones and old ones, before crossing himself and, without a word or a rearward glance, entered the mission. Above the altar was a life-size carving of Christ, and, whoever the carver had been, no one could deny that he had worked with an inspired talent. Father Damion had wondered often during Mass, when most villagers knelt, staring at the carved statue above and behind the altar, whether those kneeling people, crossing themselves and whispering prayers, eyes fixed trance-like on the anguished and averted face of the carving, were not worshipping the statue. For a priest it was a sacrilegious thought. He prayed after having it. Nevertheless, he could not forget his earlier indoctrination which recognized that people had worshipped idols for centuries before there was a Mother Church.

Tomás Henriques led the way through dark

and musty unused rooms. He took them up worn stone steps to a room just below the bell tower. In fact, the thick rope for tolling a bell came into this room through a hole in the ceiling. There was evidence that this room was occupied. Along with a Winchester rifle, leaning in a corner, there was a pallet on the floor with more blankets under it than atop it. There were several jugs of water and two crates, one atop the other, that held food.

Lázaro had known the old man had lived for years at the mission, but exactly where he had lived, Lázaro neither knew nor had been sufficiently interested to ask. When he saw what amounted to indications that this was where Tomás lived, he was not surprised. As often as not, when Henriques appeared, he had been seen in the bell tower. Father Damion nudged Lázaro and nodded for him to follow Henriques who climbed a set of narrow, worn stairs, leading to the overhead bell housing.

Everything was in place, except that there was no bell. The yoke was in place, the rope that went through the floor, a pair of stone mallets held to their handles by rawhide wrapping, even a fading set of directions on a wall about when the bell was to be rung. From the bell tower one could see for miles in all directions. There had been a time when the bell had been rung and people came from miles in all directions.

Tomás looked at the priest. 'Do you know what happened to the bell?'

'No.'

'When all the missions were sold or abandoned, soldiers took the bells to be melted down into bullets. When I was a child, my grandfather told me this. He also told me that when a bell was brought up here again, there would be a celebration, that San Ildefonso would be a village reborn.

Lázaro considered the old man. 'You had a purpose in bringing us up here?'

The old man crossed to the thick west wall, and, while his back was to his companions, he leaned over, did something Lázaro and Father Damion could not see, then faced around, holding two hands full of nicked and dull very old bars of gold.

No one spoke. Father Damion reached for one bar and examined it closely before facing Lázaro to speak. 'It is almost pure. There are specks of impurities that there would be, if whoever melted it into bars ignored bits of red and blue stones. Look.'

Lázaro accepted the bar. He was surprised at its weight and faced around until he had good light. As he was doing this, Father Damion addressed Tomás Henriques. 'Is there more?'

'Sí, much more. I can only reach into the hiding place for as long as my arm will go. Here, look.'

Father Damion went closer, saw the hole, and warily put his arm down it. Whatever he encountered, he brought up into the light and softly said: 'Sainted Mother. Lázaro...?'

The priest was holding another bar of gold, this one also with impurities. Lázaro looked but did not take the second bar. He raised his eyes to Tomás. 'How much have you taken out?'

'Enough. I put it all back.'

'How much is there, Tomás?'

'¿Quién sabe? This I can tell you. I opened the wall down in my room, and whatever was put in here went all the way down there, too, and deeper. I opened a few more holes in the wall, and always I replaced them with mud.'

Lázaro sought something to sit on. There was nothing, not even the customary bench. He placed his gold bar on a tiny shelf and spoke to the priest. 'I have to guess. That map ... the part we could read ... was written over later with dark ink.'

The priest nodded. 'The Oteros again. They made it plain to convince others the gold was here, so the word spread, and we were attacked. I would guess those soldiers of Mexico may have heard, too. As a ruse it was very good.'

'Not for the Otero brothers,' Tomás said dryly. 'They are close to the farthest boundary of the mission graveyard.'

The priest was briefly silent before speaking again. 'We'll have to open the wall all the way,' he said. 'Lázaro?'

'What?'

'What can one do with old Spanish gold?'

'Take it to Albuquerque or Santa Fé, Father, and sell it.'

'And do what with the money?'

Lázaro had no immediate answer, but Henriques had one. He'd had a long time to consider this. He said: 'Father, it is San Ildefonso's gold.'

'Tomás...?'

'San Ildefonso has lost everything these past days. Others want to leave like the Jew did. There has never been anything except water to keep people here, and you can't spend water like you can money. I should explain to you, Father. Twice I had answers to my prayers. Not for forgiveness, which I asked for and never got, but twice I was told inside my head to go above my room and break open the west wall. Father, it was God's will, unless you don't believe in such things as I didn't, until I broke into the wall. *Father, there is a God!*'

Father Damion crossed himself.

Lázaro changed the subject. 'We must have absolute secrecy between the three of us, otherwise, if this is known, the village could be attacked again. Tomás, we need tools.'

'They are down in the cells where we

brought up the cannon. I have some *martillos* under my bedding. For me, those have been enough.'

Father Damion led the way down, not to Henriques's room but all the way down to the chapel where he and the old man knelt to pray, and after a moment of hesitation Lázaro Guardia joined them.

Then Father Damion took them to his living quarters, placed a round loaf of bread on the table, and beside it a jug of wine. As he was doing this, he asked a practical question. 'How do we get the treasure to Albuquerque?'

'With the *gringo's* wagon,' Lázaro replied, breaking off a chunk of bread. 'Put the treasure in boxes spiked shut.'

'He will ask questions, Lázaro, and, if he does, then there will be others.'

El jefe leaned back. 'Load the wagon in the night. If the *gringo* has to have answers, we can give them to him after we reach Albuquerque.'

They sipped the wine and ate bread in long silence. Eventually Henriques rose. 'I'll open the hole as far down as it goes. Father, tonight the three of us can take the treasure to your room and hide it.'

'Where?'

'Under your cot, cover it with blankets. No one goes to your private place.'

As the three of them prepared to leave,

Lázaro said: 'Where did they get so much gold?'

The priest could answer. 'From Indian villages. From the mining places where the Indians got it. From attacking Indian *rancherías*. I've seen the old journals. They carried not only the banner of Spain but also the sacred cross. They took oaths to bring the true faith to heathens, but they rarely made converts. I think this was so because they cared less for making converts than they cared for finding gold.'

Tomás and the priest stayed behind to open the mud wall. Lázaro returned to the village. He was in his cubbyhole office at the corral yard when Pat Flaherty and William arrived. They looked soiled, sweaty, and tired. The freighter wanted to buy some rolled barley for his animals. Lázaro had little to spare. His supply derived from the stage company and was not his to sell, so he filled two buckets and refused to accept payment. He asked the freighter when he would expect to leave, and Flaherty winked at his shadow as he replied. 'We worked hard, got the bent axle straightened, and have the warped wheel soaking. I think we'll be ready by tomorrow. I'll be glad to leave this place.' Flaherty raised and lowered his shoulders. Without realizing it, he was beginning to act more Mexican than *gringo*. He asked why Lázaro was interested in his departure, and Lázaro lied.

'I have heard some of those who wish to leave will require a large wagon to haul their belongings in.'

Flaherty frowned slightly, then shrugged again. 'I can haul their gatherings as far as Albuquerque. Beyond that I'll need commercial freight.' Flaherty rubbed a stubby chin. 'I ain't heard no talk of folks leavin'.'

'You've been fixing the wagon.'

As the day waned, Lázaro went restlessly out to his corral to fork feed. While he was doing this, Tomás Alvarez came to lean on the mud wall as he admired the horses and said: 'I was glad I could run my wild horses over the top of those bastards, but it's not often a mustanger can catch as many as sixty head. They would have bought beans for the rest of the year. Lázaro, there is talk of abandoning the village. I think it is time. San Ildefonso has only its past. It has no future. If there was money here, or even a spur line from the railroad...'

Lázaro returned to his office with Maria Alvarez's son following. As each man sat, Lázaro said: 'And you, too, will leave?'

Tomás gazed at the floor. 'I have to. I might not have thought of it ... if I hadn't lost those wild horses.'

'You saved San Ildefonso,' Lázaro told the mustanger for the second time and was answered in the same manner as Tomás Alvarez had used before.

'It had to be done, and I knew how to do it, but trapping more wild horses will take much time and a lot of sweat. I've heard there are other places farther west where horses number into the thousands.'

Lázaro smiled. 'And you believe that?'

'Maybe not, but even if they number into the hundreds, a man may not have to ride so long and hard to catch them.'

Tomás Alvarez left with dusk settling. Lázaro intended to go to the *cantina* first. Later he would go up to the church, but not until people would be at supper. Rafael Cardinál, noticeably limping, met Lázaro in front of the shuttered windows of the abandoned general store. He had heard by way of *huaracha* telegraph that the Mejia revolution had collapsed and that now, with the insurgents fleeing in small bands, the federal troops were hunting them down with some success, but the real executioners were the hard-riding and merciless *Rurales*.

Whatever turmoil existed south of the border, Rafael Cardinál expressed the opinion that by now the insurgents had heard that General Tapia had met the *norteamericano* Army and had been sent back disarmed, and the *norteamericano* Army was near the border in force. Rafael Cardinál believed even *guerrilleros*, full of tequila, would not cross the border, and Lázaro Guardia thought he was right. He, too, had lived all his life in an area

250

where the law came from the muzzle of a gun, and only fools believed otherwise and became careless.

Rafael told Lázaro that Isabel Montenegro would sit without lighting a candle, that his own wife had talked herself hoarse without any luck. Isabel Montenegro was just too sunken in grief to listen to anyone.

The sun was still slightly above the horizon, but it was getting more red by the minute. Lázaro went across to the Montenegro house. From there he could see to the northeast where the mission stood.

Isabel came out to the shade of her *ramada*, saw Lázaro, and woodenly nodded. He went into the shade and sat on an old bench. Isabel Montenegro said – 'I have cousins in Mexico.' – and sat nearby without looking at Lázaro Guardia. 'I have another cousin married to a *gringo* cowman in Colorado. I can't stay here. Everywhere I see José.'

Lázaro leaned with clasped hands between his knees. 'He was very proud of you, and this was his village.' When the woman neither moved nor looked at him, Lázaro also said: 'Do you remember Lillian Pacheco?'

'Yes. She died too young.'

'Did you know we were going to be married?'

'Yes. It was said.' Isabel turned a dark-eyed look at Lázaro. 'This is San Ildefonso, *jefe*. If they aren't all related, they still know everyone else's business.'

Lázaro made a wry smile as he nodded.

For a moment Isabel Montenegro's gaze lingered. 'So you know what it is to lose someone?'

'Yes.'

'She was very lovely. After she died, her family moved to Santa Fé. Too many memories, *jefe*.'

Lázaro raised up to put his back to the wall. 'I wish you would stay,' he said without looking at Isabel, and she turned slowly to look at him. He considered the roadway, the adobe buildings, and sat relaxed.

She finally spoke. 'Even if I got married again, each time I passed the *cantina,* or the store, or even your corral yard, I would see José.' She abruptly looked away as she changed the subject. 'Do you know Mexico is ruining itself again?'

'Yes. Rafael told me. Don't go down there, Isabel.'

'I won't. I could, but there is so much senseless killing down there. I'll go north.'

'What will you do up north?'

'I am a good cook, Lázaro.'

He nodded. For a fact she was an excellent cook. No one, not even Fulgencio Aramas, knew so many ways to make corn and beans taste like something as rare as good beef. It was said of her that she could make burro meat taste like chicken, and Lázaro believed it. He said: 'That's *gringo* country, Isabel. If you must go somewhere, stay in the South-west.'

'I have visited up there. Yes, it is *gringo* country, but our people are up there, too. They have been there a long time. They have towns with Spanish names ... Lázaro?'

'Yes.'

'Why do you stay?'

'I was born here, so were my parents and grandparents. There have been Guardias in San Ildefonso since...'

'Is that a reason?' she asked. 'What we lived through over the past weeks ... for what? To risk being killed? Except for those rifles we would have been wiped out.'

He rose. Isabel Montenegro was a stubborn woman. If she hadn't been, she would have left José years ago. Shadows were thickening as he stood, looking down at the woman. 'Would you believe me if I told you San Ildefonso will shortly be better than it has ever been?'

She looked up. 'No.'

He left her to head for the mission. He did not hurry. The slower he walked and the more he thought, the more he became intrigued with an idea.

At the mission there were four lighted candles. The priest had shed his coat and collar. He was rumpled and sweating. Tomás Henriques eyed Lázaro, wiped off sweat, and jerked his head as he said: 'Come.' He led the way, with Father Damion bringing up the rear. When they entered the holy man's room, where two candles made light, Henriques stepped aside and said nothing. Father Damion went to a small bench and collapsed on it. Priests, by the very nature of their calling, were saved from manual labor.

Lázaro approached the iron cot against the north wall and scarcely breathed. The Spanish hoard filled the cot and had been piled high.

The priest said: 'Much more than I expected. Those *gachupínes* must have plundered in every direction for hundreds of miles. Look, you, there are even gold cups and jeweled crucifixes. Nothing was sacred, then, to those cross bearers.'

Lázaro touched nothing as he stood staring. Tomás Henriques broke the silence. 'Look under the bed, Lázaro. We could get no more on top.'

Lázaro did not look under the bed. He looked for something to sit on.

Tomás had a question. 'Can you guess how much all this will bring in *gringo* dollars?'

Lázaro couldn't and slowly shook his head. Like his companions he'd had no idea. He had anticipated perhaps several more gold bars and possibly loose coin, all crude items. What he now saw made him wonder if the old Spaniards had not been pure and simple

254

robbers, otherwise why would there be golden chalices from churches and great crucifixes of the kind he had seen in Albuquerque?

Tomás Henriques provided an answer to his own question. 'A fortune, Lázaro. A very great fortune.'

The holy man roused out of his exhaustion to mumble about the weight. He had made a dozen trips from the cache to his room, weighed down with treasure. His knowledge of gold was limited to what he had seen in holy places – candlesticks, crosiers, altar ornaments, massive solid gold covers for Bibles. He said: 'I had no idea gold was so heavy.'

Tomás produced a bottle, filled three cups, and handed them around, keeping the fullest one for himself. There was a long period of silence before the oldest man among them spoke dryly, candlelight showing his lined face in shadowy light. 'I will say to you what this means to me ... the only opportunity I shall ever have to pay for my years of sin.'

This was too good an opportunity for the priest to let it pass. He remembered Henriques's denunciation at Maria Alvarez's grave. 'Why then,' he asked, 'do you suppose the Lord told you where the treasure was, not once, but twice? Why, Tomás? To provide you with the means for doing ten right things for every wrong thing you did.'

Lázaro barely heard. He rose as he said: 'It must be crated. The *gringo's* wagon will be ready to leave San Ildefonso by tomorrow. Tomás, are there crates here?'

'None that I know of,' he replied.

'Then we must...'

'At Morisco's store,' Tomás interrupted to say. 'Not only out back but inside. If we take them, it must be now, in the dark. Father...?'

'Yes, of course. Let me rest a little.'

Chapter Seventeen

Albuquerque

In a place where people bedded down early in order to save candles, Lázaro Guardia, the priest, and Tomás Henriques had to wait impatiently. Even then, as they went down the alley as far as the store, some idiot was playing a lachrymose song of lost love on his guitar that would be guaranteed to keep people awake, particularly wives with great lumps of masculinity snoring at their sides.

Tomás was seemingly tireless. After their fourth trip to the village and back, the priest rested in the pleasant night out back where he gave thanks for the crates and also requested more energy. His prayer of gratitude was acknowledged, his request for energy was not.

There were not enough crates, so Lázaro and the old man improvised, using ancient canvas, even blankets off the holy man's cot. The crates were heavy, and the bundles unwieldy, but, when they finished and went out back to the *ramada,* Father Damion was stretched out, sound asleep on the only bench, so they sat on the edge of the *ramada*

257

where generations of feet had made the adobe paving uneven.

Tomás had a question. 'Those *bandoleros* who fled northward will be somewhere up ahead?'

Lázaro's reply suggested that *el jefe* had considered this. 'We need Juan Bohorquez, Tomás Alvarez, Rafael Cardinál, and maybe two or three more, all with guns. They can be what the *gringos* call outriders.'

'It will be dawn before long. Do you want me to go with you for those men?'

'No, Tomás. Stay here. When the priest is rested, the pair of you bring the crates and bundles to the south end of the *ramada*. That is where the *gringo* can back his wagon and let down the tailgate.'

Henriques considered a callused hand. He had an idea that Father Damion would be of little use – and that meant *he* would have to bring the treasure to the *ramada* by himself. He sighed, '*Jefe*, I wonder if there isn't an easier way to serve the Lord.'

Lázaro brushed the old man's shoulder as he rose to walk back to the village.

It was dark, the moon was gone, and a dog barked somewhere as Lázaro sought the freighter's camp. It was easily found. There was only one big freight wagon. Flaherty and William were making breakfast over a tiny fire encased in a stone ring. When Lázaro appeared, the freighter looked up quizzically. 'Coffee?' he asked as Lázaro squatted, shaking his head.

'There is a load up at the mission for you to haul to Albuquerque.'

Flaherty gazed steadily at Lázaro over the rim of a dented tin cup. 'When?' he asked.

'Now. As soon as you finish here and can put harness on your animals.'

Flaherty drank down to the dregs and flung the residue into the little fire as he began: '*Jefe...?*'

'It is urgent.'

They gazed steadily at each other for a long moment before the freighter told William to bring in the mules.

As Lázaro turned to depart, he told Flaherty to back his wagon to the edge of the long *ramada,* that there would be help waiting.

Arousing Juan Bohorquez from a sound sleep in the lean-to of his *cantina* where he lived was not as easy. The burly man leaned up off his cot with a six-gun pointing. He said: 'What is it? Do you know what time it is?'

Lázaro explained what he wanted, told the saloonman to ride to the south end of the *ramada,* told him there had to be others. The last thing he said was– 'Bring your guns.' –and left the saloonman, who was not yet fully awake.

Rousing Rafael Cardinál brought a problem. His wife, more acute than her husband, agreed that she and her man would saddle horses at once and go to the mission. After saying this, she also said: 'Is it more *bandidos, jefe?*'

Lázaro squirmed. 'No, it is to escort the *gringo's* big wagon northward.'

'You have contraband?' she asked.

'No, *señora*. I am in a hurry.'

The woman's next remark was faintly sarcastic. 'Yes, of course, you are in a hurry. Why shouldn't you be, arousing people in their beds to do something about which you do not explain.'

Lázaro found Tomás Alvarez making breakfast in his mother's *jacal* and said only that he needed the mustanger to escort Flaherty's wagon north. Tomás Alvarez accepted the remark as though he was accustomed to doing things about which he was told nothing. He said he would saddle his horse and ride to the mission.

Dawn was coming. Lázaro hesitated. He wanted more armed outriders, but maybe those he had were enough. He returned to the mission where Patrick Flaherty darkly regarded him. The wagon was nearly loaded, but the *gringo* said nothing. By the time the others arrived, including Rafael's wife armed to the gills, Flaherty and the boy had climbed to the high seat. Flaherty kicked the binders loose and talked up his hitch. Tomás rode in back. The priest joined Lázaro in returning to the village for horses they got at the stage company's corral yard. As they rode up through the village, where breakfast fires sent smoke from chimneys, Father Damion said: 'I would feel better if we had soldiers with us.'

Lázaro did not reply.

When the sun came over the far eastern curve of the world, the cavalcade was well along, raising a little dust, animals snorting now and then, and a blessed coolness making life easy for creatures who would have little ease after the sun climbed higher. They made excellent time, which was fortunate because they had many miles to cover. The freighter called a halt near midday when they encountered one of those stone troughs beside the road that were fed from distant sump springs through hollowed saplings.

As was customary, they had to fight off hordes of irate mud daubers to water the animals and themselves. It was at this place Flaherty confronted Lázaro Guardia. 'The old man was trying to load by himself. The priest was lying flat out on a bench. Tell me, friend, if I am right or wrong. The only thing I know of that can outweigh me in small crates is gold.'

Lázaro was saved from having to answer

by the lad on the high seat with his rifle between his knees. He called to Flaherty: 'Riders comin' from out yonder.'

The dust was not high, but it was moving. Rafael, bridling his mount after it had tanked up, said: 'I count six.'

His wife exerted the feminine right to make a contradiction. 'Eight!'

Flaherty, instinctively obeying an old soldier's training and experience, said: 'Get a-horseback. *Jefe*, you lead the charge.'

Juan Bohorquez, already astride, scowled at the freighter. 'We don't know who they are.'

Flaherty replied without taking his eyes off the approaching riders. 'We don't have to know. All they have to know is that we are armed.'

Francesca was astride when her husband told her to stay with the wagon and the boy. She would have protested, if the mounted men hadn't whirled in a leap, heading for the distant horsemen. Tomás also remained with the wagon. She turned to him but he ignored her.

The distant riders pulled down to a halt, watching the men with the wagon coming straight for them, with one or two balancing Winchesters in their laps. The strangers were grouped until one of them spoke, after which they abruptly turned and fled.

Lázaro did not follow. He sat his animal,

watching them raise more dust as they fled.

Rafael, with only one foot in the stirrup so he could favor his injured ankle, said: *Guerrilleros*, Lázaro.'

Flaherty spat and turned back. He said nothing until they were again with the wagon, then he eased up beside Lázaro, softly said– 'Very heavy.' –and then led his animal away.

As the sun set, they followed the freighter's advice, left the road, and continued until they saw creek willows. Flaherty had camped at this place where there was water many times. They hobbled the animals. Francesca supervised the making of a meal. The freighter said he and William would take the first watch.

There was very little conversation as they ate or afterwards. Juan, Rafael, and Flaherty were almost sullen in their regard of the priest, Tomás Henriques, and Lázaro Guardia.

The second day they hadn't been on the road more than three hours when William told Flaherty he could see a wagon in the distance. Flaherty squinted, saw nothing, and pretended that he had, but the lad was right. With the sun slanting away, they overtook the solitary traveler up ahead. It was Moses Morisco. He was more surprised to see them, armed to the teeth, than they were to see him. After greetings had been exchanged, he asked their destination. Lázaro said it was

Albuquerque, but, when the storekeeper asked other questions, Lázaro smiled and rode ahead. Moses Morisco asked questions of the others. Tomás Henriques was the only one who answered, and his replies added to the mystery rather than otherwise. Tomás said: 'You stay with us. When we go back to San Ildefonso, you will understand.'

Whoever those unidentified riders of the day before had been, they were never to know for certain. Although a guard was kept far back, the strangers did not reappear. Flaherty, as a former soldier, confided in William that those riders had been marauders. He knew this from the way they rode, and how they had fled in the face of a charge in their direction by armed riders from the wagon.

William surprised Flaherty by saying: 'When we haul freight, will we run into more like them?'

Flaherty eyed the boy, who had made up his mind he wanted to be a freighter, too, and only shrugged.

When they had Albuquerque in sight, it was close to day's end. Lázaro and Juan Bohorquez left the others in camp and rode to the city. Francesca said aloud they would arrive when all the stores were closed, and no one contradicted her. For the *gringo* freighter, somewhere up ahead he would unload, find another haul, say good bye to the others, and with William resume a way of life he enjoyed

– always moving, seeing new country, meeting people, and sedulously avoiding contact with soldiers and Army posts.

It was midnight or close to it when Juan and Lázaro returned with a stranger, riding between them, and now, for the first time, the people who had only guessed at the cargo stood dumbfounded in moonlight as reflection from their dying supper fire bounced off gold bars once Lázaro opened one of the bundles. The stranger was a hard-eyed, mostly expressionless individual who put Francesca Cardinál in mind of a vulture. He climbed into the wagon to help Lázaro and Juan open other bundles and crates. The stranger removed his hat, mopped off sweat, and sat on a crate. Lázaro said: 'Did I lie?'

The stranger from Albuquerque shook his head. 'Are you sure it's not stolen?'

'Only from Spaniards who must be dead a hundred years.'

The stranger rose, rummaged through the bundles and crates, and sat down again. 'Is there more?' he asked.

Lázaro shook his head, then asked a question of his own. 'Have you seen enough to make a price?'

The stranger blew out a long breath before answering.

'Mister, I doubt there's enough cash money in all of Albuquerque to pay for all this.' He then seemed to have a second thought. 'But I can raise it. I have contacts. What do you think it is worth?'

Lázaro spread his hands. 'I know nothing of these things.'

The stranger's gaze clung to *el jefe's* face. 'I will give you five thousand dollars right now, tonight. We'll ride back to the city, and I'll...'

Francesca interrupted. 'Three times that much, *señor*. And more. We'll go into the city in the morning. There will be others who will buy gold.'

The stranger considered Rafael's wife. The boldness of her gaze and the set of her jaw made him reconsider the treasure around him. 'Maybe a little more, ma'am, but it all has to be melted down and the impurities taken out. That costs money.'

Francesca's gaze at the sweating stranger did not waver. 'Fifteen thousand, *señor.*'

'I'll have to raise the money, and it can't be done in one day.'

Francesca raised the ante. 'Eighteen thousand, *señor.*'

The stranger transferred his gaze to Lázaro, who simply shrugged. Father Damion approached the tailgate and stood beside Francesca Cardinál. He asked the stranger his name.

'Jonas Frost, Father.'

'Mister Frost, how many money-changers are there in Albuquerque?'

266

'I don't know, Father.'

'But more than one, Mister Frost? In the morning we could drive the wagon into the city and find others who buy gold.'

Frost narrowed his eyes at the priest. 'Father, all I'd have to do is pass word that this hoard is stolen, and you wouldn't be able to sell one bar of...'

The pistols which appeared and were cocked in the night stopped Frost's voice. He could see some of them but not all. On the high seat a youth was resting a long-barreled rifle on the wood at his back. When he cocked the thing, the barrel was less than five feet from Jonas Frost's head, and the sound of the rifle being cocked carried well beyond the wagon.

Pat Flaherty went as far as the tailgate, but Moses Morisco climbed over the tailgate and went from crate to crate before sitting on one as he quietly addressed Frost: 'My grandfather was a money-changer in Portugal. Before that, he worked in Spain. He taught me some things. In Albuquerque there must be an assayer. He can tell us within a few dollars what this old Spanish hoard is worth. Mister Frost, do you know an assayer?'

Frost scowled at old Moses Morisco. 'Far as I know, there ain't no assayer in Albuquerque.'

Moses smiled. 'Maybe in Santa Fé? It isn't much farther north.'

267

Frost's eyes hardened on Morisco. 'When word spreads about you folks, drivin' around the country with what you got in this wagon, you'll be lucky to be alive to reach Santa Fé.'

Juan Bohorquez climbed into the wagon, faced Frost, and said: 'You're the only one who knows, and, if I break your neck, no one will know.'

Lázaro didn't like the way this discussion was going, so he addressed the man from Albuquerque. 'Eighteen thousand *norteamericano* dollars and we will hitch up and go back with you.'

Frost was briefly silent, then said: 'Sixteen thousand. Do you know how much money that is? It can buy whole towns.'

Lázaro's reply was short. 'We will go back with you and wait in the morning for the money.'

'Sixteen thousand?'

Lázaro nodded. Beyond the tailgate people stood like statues. Those who had worked in their lives for no more than fifteen dollars a month could not grasp the idea of sixteen thousand dollars. It was riches beyond their dreams. When Flaherty and his shadow went after the mules, Tomás Henriques accompanied them. When the mules were being fitted with lead shanks and were afterwards freed of their hobbles, Tomás told the freighter the man from Albuquerque had to be a liar. There was not that much money in all of New Mexico Territory, and Pat Flaherty told the older man of armored mine wagons, transporting that much money every year.

Jonas Frost sat in deep thought even after the wagon was moving with his saddle animal tied to the tailgate. When they were on the outskirts of Albuquerque, he spoke to Juan Bohorquez and the priest, the only others riding on the wagon seat. He asked how they had found the Spanish cache, and neither man answered him. He then asked where it had been found.

The priest said: 'San Ildefonso. It is a long story. There is an old map, saying it was in San Luis Rey. Two men named Otero had the map. I think they wrote on it for people to think the cache was at San Luis Rey, which would have gotten the marauders from Mexico to go north, so the Otero brothers would not be bothered while they searched in San Ildefonso.'

'Where are those Otero brothers?'

'Dead, Mister Frost.'

'Who besides you people know of the treasure?'

'No one, I think. Tell me, Mister Frost, what will you do with it?'

'Melt it down into bars.'

'And sell it?'

Jonas Frost gazed at the priest as though the holy man was neither a child nor an idiot. 'What else would I do with it?'

'For a profit, Mister Frost?'

The man from Albuquerque not only didn't answer, he avoided even looking at the priest. Juan Bohorquez had a question. 'Will we have to wait while you get the money, *señor?*'

This time Frost's exasperation showed clearly. 'Do you think I have sixteen thousand dollars in my store? Do you know what a bank is?'

Juan nodded.

'That's where I'll have to get it.' Frost paused while regarding Juan Bohorquez. 'Do you know where there might be another old Spanish cache?'

Juan smiled as he shook his head.

Frost gave Flaherty directions after they reached the sprawling outskirts of Albuquerque. Daylight was not far off, and there were people on the roadways. A few stopped to watch the wagon pass with its heavily armed escort, but mostly the cavalcade drew no attention. Albuquerque had been the seat of overland trade for a hundred years. Big wagons were no novelty. Where Jonas Frost guided Flaherty to the front of a large store, and Flaherty applied the binders, Jonas Frost said: 'Wait here. It will be a couple of hours before the bank is open. Don't talk to anyone. Don't let anyone see what's in the wagon. *¿Comprende?*'

The outriders dismounted and tied their horses to the long rack in front of the store where they saw the very large, ornate sign saying: **J. Frost, Mercantile.**

Lázaro came to the rack to loop his reins, saw the sign, and told the others he had been told by several people in the Mexican section of town that *Señor* Frost was the richest man in New Mexico, and Lázaro had hunted him down, routed him from bed, and they knew the rest of the story.

As they waited, the sun climbed. Moses Morisco took his old wagon horse to a shady place where he brought buckets of water and even some grain he had bought from a liveryman. As time passed and curious people stood in small groups, eyeing the wagon, but mostly the heavily armed people with it, and in particular the woman wearing crossed bandoleers, the new day's heat began to arrive.

When Jonas Frost returned, he had four strong men with him. He gave the orders that began the unloading. The strong men had evidently been instructed to say nothing, only to carry the crates and bundles into Frost's store.

Lázaro's companions watched all this and went with *el jefe* to surround Jonas Frost. He handed Lázaro a piece of paper and told him, if he wanted to cash the check, to go to the bank, which Lázaro did, accompanied by his unsmiling, heavily armed companions.

There were two *gringos* waiting. Without a word they took Frost's piece of paper and handed Lázaro a bulging leather satchel. One of them, an older, bald individual, said: 'Count it if you like. It's all there.'

Juan Bohorquez smiled at the bald man without a shred of humor. 'If it isn't, *amigo*, we will come back and cut off, first your ears, then your nose, then the tongue.'

The bald man moved farther away, and the other *gringo* told Lázaro, if he deposited the money in the bank, he could write checks against his deposit. He also said it was not only foolish, it was also dangerous to leave Albuquerque with that much money.

Lázaro agreed with him and left the bank, carrying the satchel. Flaherty met them. He was ready to go north in search of trade. Lázaro invited him to a café before he left. He also invited Moses Morisco. An hour later, with the sun almost directly overhead while they were eating, Lázaro said he wanted to hire Flaherty for the drive back to San Ildefonso, and Flaherty darkly scowled. 'Hire me to go back there ... why?'

'Because Moses Morisco's wagon can't carry all that he'll need to restock his store.'

Moses Morisco's eyes widened at Lázaro. 'What are you saying?'

'I'm saying that San Ildefonso would have lost to the border marauders, except for you, among others. We will go with you to where you get supplied. You will take what you need, and we will pay for it. Moses, we need you in San Ildefonso. We need Pat Flaherty to haul all your things for the store.'

Three diners at the café stopped eating to listen and stare. Even the caféman came from his cooking area. Moses Morisco didn't finish his meal. He did something no one had ever seen him do before. He bought a cigar, lighted it, and went out to the plank walk to watch people, rigs of all kinds, and riders pass.

When the others came out, he told them where the supply house was and left his old horse in shade, climbed to the high seat of Flaherty's freighter, sat next to William, and savored the cigar as he gave directions. Behind him the others rode on horseback.

Chapter Eighteen

Questions And Some Answers

It required more than an hour for Moses Morisco to pass his needs on to a portly, bald man with pale blue eyes. Part way through the process, as crates were being put into Flaherty's wagon, the paunchy bald man asked how he would be paid. Lázaro placed the satchel atop the counter and opened it. The pale-eyed man looked and drew back slowly. 'What else, Mister Morisco?'

When all that would be needed to re-supply San Ildefonso's only mercantile had been loaded, the portly man stood under his shaded overhang to watch. He said nothing, did not even wave, as Flaherty talked up his hitch.

Lázaro watched store fronts until he saw one in particular and asked Flaherty to hold up a few minutes. Lázaro entered the store that only had one window, facing the roadway, and was gloomy inside. This time the storekeeper was a turkey-necked *gringo* with an unruly thatch, shot through with gray, and a long nose. He was working on a shotgun when Lázaro approached the counter with a question. 'Where can I buy a Gatling gun?'

The lanky man's Adam's apple bobbed twice. He looked steadily at Lázaro as he said: 'Mister, Gatling guns belong to the Army. You can't just waltz into a gun shop and buy one.'

'Some raiders up out of Mexico who attacked our town had one.'

'What village, mister?'

'San Ildefonso.'

The gunsmith nodded slightly. 'I was down there once, years back. Ain't nothin' there but mud houses.'

'How much would a Gatling gun cost?' Lázaro asked.

'The Army don't sell 'em. I expect, like your raiders, they get stole and sold, but...'

'How much, *señor.*'

The shock-headed man studied Lázaro as he answered: 'I'd guess maybe as much as two hunnert *gringo* dollars.'

'Would three hundred *gringo* dollars buy one and ammunition for it?'

The gunsmith wiped both hands on a greasy apron before saying: 'No, mister, but four hunnert *gringo* dollars would. You ever seen that much money?'

Lázaro put the satchel on the counter and opened it. The gunsmith's eyes bulged. 'Counterfeit, is it?'

'No. Do you know Jonas Frost?'

'Everyone knows Mister Frost. Is that

where you got the money?'

'Yes.'

The gunsmith wiped his hands again as Lázaro closed the satchel. Finally, the gunsmith jerked his head and led the way to a large storage room where a dust-covered Gatling stood with a long clip atop it and another clip on the earthen floor beside it. The gunsmith lowered his voice. 'It's yours, mister, providin' you give me your word you won't never say where you got it.'

Lázaro counted our four hundred dollars and went outside to beckon Juan Bohorquez and Pat Flaherty. When they saw the gun, they stood like statues. Eventually Flaherty had a question for the gunsmith. 'Where'd you get it?'

The gunsmith considered Flaherty. 'Your friend here just bought it. That's all you got to know.'

Without another word Flaherty went outside to lower the tailgate and jerked his head for Tomás Alvarez and Juan Bohorquez to follow him.

It required an hour to disassemble the gun and carry it in pieces to the wagon. The steel-shod wheels were almost as heavy as the multi-barreled muzzle. When it was loaded, Flaherty yanked the tailgate chains and latched them. Lázaro nodded to the gunsmith and went to the horse Francesca Cardinál was holding for him. As he mounted, expecting the woman to speak, she got astride her own animal without opening her mouth.

Tomás Henriques and Father Damion spoke almost in whispers as Flaherty turned the wagon and started southward out of Albuquerque. Juan Bohorquez rode stirrup with Lázaro Guardia, trying to think of a tactful way of asking questions and failed. Juan Bohorquez had been born with attributes, but tact was not one of them. He and Lázaro rode in silence until Albuquerque was no longer in sight, and then it wasn't Juan who asked a question, it was Rafael Cardinál. He had been told to do so by his wife, and Lázaro replied matter-of-factly: 'If the *guerrilleros* had one, then there had to be others, because they don't make them in Mexico, and Albuquerque is a large place.'

'But did you know that gunsmith?'

Father Damion spoke. 'He didn't have to know the gunsmith.'

That settled the discussion until they were again camping where they had camped on the way north. Then Lázaro explained, and only Juan Bohorquez commented. 'This was in your head?'

'San Ildefonso will be able to protect itself, if the raiders come again and if we place the gun facing southward where they can see it...'

Juan smiled widely, stopped only when Tomás nudged him, and offered a bottle.

Francesca Cardinál frowned. 'Where did you get that, *viejo?*'

Tomás Henriques looked her in the eyes when he answered. 'Albuquerque is a place of miracles, *señora*. Look, we have a crank gun. No one else will have such a thing.'

'I'm not talking about the crank gun!'

Tomás was taking back the bottle when he spoke again. 'If strangers can come into Albuquerque and buy a crank gun, do you think it would be impossible to buy a bottle of *pulque* on the street?'

They broke camp before sunrise and were well on their way before they noticed great white-cloud galleons, moving with infinite slowness from the northeast. No one had wet-weather clothing for an excellent reason. It never rained during the hottest month of the year. It rained in the springtime and during the south desert's brief winter, but rarely otherwise. Nevertheless, as they traveled, the immense bank of white clouds continued to move, and people whose lives had been spent in desert country had no illusions about the contents of those huge clouds.

They arrived late at their second camping place where the mud daubers were busily taking wet earth to wherever they had their village and did not appreciate being interrupted. They saw the last of the stinging varmints just about the time dusk arrived.

Flaherty and his partner worried, mostly in silence. Flaherty had told William word would spread like wildfire about strangers, accompanying a freight wagon southward with a satchel full of *gringo* dollars. Flaherty was not the only worried person. Francesca, for example, insisted that everyone remain awake, and that someone should go back and watch for night riders. Tomás Henriques volunteered after he heard Maria Alvarez's son volunteer. Father Damion watched them leave, each with a saddle gun as well as a holstered Colt.

Francesca had to rummage for food. When she passed around tin plates, because everyone was hungry, they cleaned them down to the metal without comment. Rafael's wife waited, hands on hips, for them to finish.

Once, after the moon was beginning its descent, there was the sound of horsemen. Henriques told Tomás Alvarez he thought they were going the wrong way. It sounded like they were heading for Albuquerque. Nevertheless, the mustanger jerked his head for the old man to follow, and they scouted.

When they returned, Francesca passed tin plates to them with what was left over from the meal. It wasn't much, but neither one complained. After this, there was a general discussion. There should be a committee to agree, or disagree, on what the money was to be spent on. No one mentioned Lázaro's purchase of the crank gun or the supplies for Morisco's store. They all would have agreed about those things. Father Damion was appointed head of the committee. Francesca was also appointed, as were Lázaro and Juan Bohorquez. Rafael Cardinál, Tomás Henriques, and the mustanger were not appointed which did not seem to bother them. They were more worried about those banks of massive clouds. Only after they were again on the southward road did Lázaro say he did not believe the storm was traveling south, and he was correct. When it broke loose, it nearly swamped Albuquerque. The residual effect was a cooling light wind that brightened the spirits of the wagoners and even Flaherty's mules which quickened their gait.

Eventually, when they had San Ildefonso in sight, the place appeared deserted. Lázaro loped ahead. He met Isabel Montenegro under her *ramada* with a hide *alforja* nearby. When Lázaro reined up and dismounted, she gave him no opportunity to speak first.

'I told you I'm going to Colorado. I have another *alforja* to pack, then I have to find an animal that carries packs.'

Lázaro spoke slowly and distinctly for several minutes. When he finished, José's widow said: 'What did you say? There's not that much money in the whole territory.'

Lázaro smiled. 'A question, Isabel. Would you stay if there was that much money for our town?'

'I'd have to see it. And then I don't know. What is there for me here? Even Fulgencio Aramas packed up and left.' She gestured with both arms. 'Look, there is nothing left, and there never was much to begin with.'

Lázaro pointed northward.

Isabel leaned forward and peered. As she leaned back, she said: 'That's the *gringo's* big wagon. He...'

'Behind is Moses Morisco. They are all coming back.'

She sniffed with either suspicion or doubt. 'Why? Moses, too? His store is empty. Everything is gone from the shelves.'

The wagon was approaching the northern outskirts of the village. Isabel Montenegro again leaned forward and frowned. 'Francesca and Rafael? How is his ankle?'

As the dusty cavalcade entered San Ildefonso, Lázaro went to the roadway and gestured for Francesca Cardinál to turn off. She did so and halted, gazing toward the porch and the *alforja* as Lázaro talked. When he finished, she looked down, nodded, and rode to the front of the house. As she was dismounting, she said: 'Is it true that great ox, Fulgencio Aramas, has left?'

'Yes. The day before yesterday. He told the Indian woman he was going to Texas.'

Francesca held the reins to her horse, considered Isabel, and said: 'He was unpleasant

281

and cooked meals only the very hungry could eat. Isabel...?'

The women looked steadily at each over a period of moments before Isabel Montenegro spoke. 'No! I am leaving.'

Francesca looked around where Lázaro was leading his horse toward the road, looked back, and said: 'San Ildefonso will grow. There is no better cook in all the territory. San Ildefonso needs you. It needs a place where people can be fed well by a good cook. Consider it, Isabel. Take my word for it, San Ildefonso will grow because, after so many generations of surviving, we now have the money to make it grow, maybe even to pay for a spur track from the railroad to here. Isabel...'

Francesca followed the route of the other woman's gaze out to where Lázaro Guardia was leading his horse southward behind the big wagon. Francesca softened her voice. 'The man who did the thinking, I believe, should be mayor ... which is better than *alcalde*.'

Isabel agreed, still watching Lázaro. When she returned her gaze to Francesca, she asked: 'Suppose Fulgencio Aramas comes back?'

'He won't. He never liked San Ildefonso or cooking. Think, Isabel. It's not just a place to eat. If you take it over, it will keep you busy, feeding people who haven't been fed well since you and I were small children. I tell you again, San Ildefonso needs you.' Francesca lowered her voice again. 'Lázaro Guardia is thin. He needs meat on his bones. You could put it there. Lázaro Guardia is a man who appreciates things. Well, I must go and take care of this animal and maybe come back this evening. I also have to find my husband.'

Isabel, who had been facing the roadway, said: 'I saw him enter the *cantina* a few minutes ago.'

Francesca turned abruptly to lead the horse where she could care for it, her back as straight as a ramrod.

Isabel watched men carry crates into Moses Morisco's store. Moses latched his bulletproof shutters open. To Isabel he seemed to have a spring in his step she hadn't seen in years.

The coolness continued. Northward, for as long as daylight lasted, it was possible to see those massive clouds, hovering about where Albuquerque was. Isabel sat down, erect and wide-eyed, while the men unloaded the Gatling gun, put the wheels onto protruding axles, and even placed the long, narrow magazine up where it belonged.

Most of the village came to stare. Isabel crossed the road. Father Damion was asked to bless the gun, which he did as Genero Salas watched disapprovingly. Before he could protest about a holy man blessing an instrument whose sole purpose was killing, Torres Mendoza loudly declared, if *guerrilleros* came and saw the gun, he doubted that they would remain, and there was laughter.

Genero Salas left the crowd, and no one missed him.

Francesca Cardinál nudged her husband. 'Move Lázaro closer to Isabel Montenegro.'

Rafael turned, scowling. 'Why should I do that? Besides, my leg is aching.'

Francesca did it herself, only she maneuvered Isabel close to one of the crank gun's wheels where Lázaro was leaning. He turned, exchanged a long, steady gaze with Isabel Montenegro and, when Francesca Cardinál said it was possible that Isabel would operate the eatery, Lázaro smiled. Francesca hovered until they were talking, then worked through the crowd, back to her husband's side. He said: 'What are you doing?'

'Isabel will run the eating place.'

Rafael considered briefly before speaking again. 'I heard she wanted to leave.'

'You can hear anything in the *cantina*. We should go home. Your leg must hurt.'

'Those of us who went north with the wagon are going to meet again later at the *cantina*.'

'You haven't had anything to eat since morning,' Francesca said, and took Rafael by the arm to lead him away.

Pat Flaherty saw this and grinned. He had

been at the *cantina* earlier where Rafael had downed three tequilas in a row.

William tugged Flaherty's sleeve. 'The mules need to be fed and cared for.'

Flaherty nodded, went to the leaders, and led them to the corral yard. William was not tall enough to unhook the traces where they went over the rump of each mule, but he helped in other ways, and Flaherty watched him in silence. For the hundredth time he wondered why William's parents had not come back for him. Neither Flaherty nor William Colson would ever know the answer.

Tomás Alvarez went to the Alvarez house. Tomás Henriques went to his room at the mission. The only person who knew of their relationship – Father Damion – was replaced as parish priest the same year the Forthright Stage & Freight Company resumed the runs to San Ildefonso. It was also the same year 'singing wires', as the Indians called them, came to San Ildefonso, along with a skinny *gringo* telegrapher to maintain contact with the outside world.

The railroad spur was never established for economic reasons, but, as the village prospered, it acquired a blacksmith and two other businesses. Lázaro's corral yard was expanded to accommodate freighters.

There came an evening in springtime when Lázaro Guardia and Isabel Montenegro leaned on his corral, looking in at the

285

animals, mostly big Missouri mules or twelve-hundred-pound horses, listening to the animal eating. Isabel asked a question.

'Has the *gringo* come back?'

'Flaherty? No. I've watched for him and waited, but no, he and William have never returned.'

'But they should, Lázaro.'

True or not, it was a statement that required no response. Lázaro asked about the café. Isabel Montenegro shrugged. 'It is doing very well,' she replied, and juggled a thought in her mind. 'Lázaro?'

'Yes.'

'I am fifty-five years old.'

He turned. 'Is that important to you?'

'I think you and I must be about the same age.'

He smiled indulgently. 'Not by ten years.'

'You are sixty-five?'

He gestured. 'There are no young people except for the Indian woman's grandchild.'

The conversation hadn't turned out as she had wanted it to. She leaned beside him, looking at the large animals without speaking. Lázaro Guardia was a good man, but as thick as oak. She said: 'Good night.'

He watched her walk away.

The publishers hope that this book has given you enjoyable reading. Large Print Books are especially designed to be as easy to see and hold as possible. If you wish a complete list of our books please ask at your local library or write directly to:

The Golden West Large Print Books
Magna House, Long Preston,
Skipton, North Yorkshire.
BD23 4ND

This Large Print Book, for people
who cannot read normal print,
is published under the auspices of

THE ULVERSCROFT FOUNDATION